D'

Bull Session

by T. Morris Longstreth

Bull Session

T. Morris Longstreth

THE MACMILLAN COMPANY • NEW YORK • 1958

Dedicated to
THOMAS SHIPLEY BROWN, JR.
outdoorsman, laughs-lover, and good friend

Contents

Bull Session

NOTICE

Those readers who tend to confuse the
faculty and students of Ironwood School
with the personnel of George School and
Westtown, should have their heads ex-
amined—and *soon*.

1 -

Preview on the Run

The time was 11:59 A.M. with sixty seconds to go before the long-awaited explosion into Christmas vacation.

The great Ironwood School sat on its snowy hill in wintry silence. But in a dozen classrooms three hundred faces watched paralyzed clocks.

Suddenly bells shrilled, gongs clanged, and the three hundred burst into freedom. Boys and girls boiled out of doorways into the quarter mile of corridor that ran the building's length. They raced (against rules) and shouted "Merry Christmas" to friends and faculty alike.

So thorough was the thaw from discipline into gaiety, that even Master Henry Vanner, dean of boys, consented not to notice Hobey Tyler's kiss of parting with Diane Ebbitt, there under the library stairs.

Into the heart of the building, called the Hall, poured two streams of vacationers from the boys' and girls' dormitories. Ninth graders lugged baggage too big for them. Excited daters sought their other halves, and parents were arriving.

Teacher Minnie Winters, dean of girls, a veteran of thirty such departings, said to Teacher Genevieve Lemaine of Paris, "You might suppose they were fleeing from certain death instead of from an education they're paying for—or asking us to."

"*Oui,* in France it is different. This is the way they run *to* school."

Celia Nash looked at Andy Bellman, who also had overheard, and framed her lips to say, "Liar!"

"Merry Christmas!" on all sides.

"Same to you!"

"Be seeing you!"

*   *   *   *   *

Actually there were three hundred happy departures less one. Savey Miller dreaded vacations, because they broke into the adventure which was Ironwood School. They meant trading the excitement of *people* for his prim little home. He loved his kind mother, his careful father. He was grateful to them for scrimping so that he could go to Ironwood. His conscience upbraided him for hating to be housed up safely in his lonely room, even for two weeks, when he might be lost in the jungles of Ironwood's coeducational arrangements. Two forlorn weeks, with no Library, no chance to look at Sid Dalton from afar, *no Teacher Lola.*

At this crushing realization, Savey went somewhat sick. Savey, in his sixteenth year, was not over worshiping Sid, the notable athlete, before he was seized with this new feeling for Lola Wilson, the assistant librarian. The mixture of emotions kept him on the rack. Now, as he bore a load of library books that must be returned, he tried to word a farewell that would say all he wished to say without giving himself away.

Savey, like most brains, overlooked unimportant matters, and now the armload of books interfered with his view. He did not notice Nick Dorritt's foot dexterously extended to trip him, and as dexterously withdrawn. Savey stumbled against Lola's desk, the books cascaded, and one landed in the place best suited to upset the ink.

"Oh, Savery!" Lola cried sympathetically, for she pitied this shy stripling with the fine blue eyes whom nobody seemed to appreciate.

"I-I d-didn't . . ."

"No, of course you didn't!" Lola interrupted understandingly.

"B-but the ink!" Savey pulled out a handkerchief.

"Don't, *don't!* That's a clean handkerchief. Wait."

Together, they stayed the ink, picked up the books, looked at each other, and Lola said, "I know you'll have a good vacation, Savery."

"I-I hope it's short." Savey's look explained.

"Oh, don't say that. I—we . . ."

"You know why I say it," Savey replied meaningfully.

"I do indeed, just so that you can come and take out twenty more books."

"You know it isn't that," Savey said and stopped. He couldn't find any more words.

*   *   *   *   *

In Room 21 on the second floor of the boys' dormitory, Vance Draper squeezed his suitcase together with an accompaniment of language unsuitable for faculty ears. Then he discovered his shaving kit left out and grew more eloquent still. With the kit stowed and the bag closed again, he remembered that he had packed the list of things that Hobey Tyler must bring back to school as his share in the dark proceedings they had planned. His face tightened with anger at himself, but he got the list. For Vance, at seventeen and a few months, was destined to go places. The dean of boys thought so, too, but they were different places.

Hobey Tyler, Vance's roommate, entered at this inopportune moment. His appearance was smug after his meeting with Diane, and it irritated Vance. He said, "Where do you think you've been?"

"I know where I've been. What's eating you?"

"Here's the list," Vance countered. "Check it before you leave home, or we'll be sunk."

Hobey, who was tall, attractive, easy-going, and trained by his parents to be socially ambitious, found it hard to accommodate himself to Vance's efficiency. He glanced at the list and exclaimed, "One white mouse! What do you think we are at home, a zoo?"

"We have to run the wires under the floor. They use white mice to do it. Or ferrets. Bring a ferret if you'd rather."

Hobey was reading further. "Two headphones! For cri . . ."

"*You* want to listen, don't you?" Vance interrupted.

"Who's paying for all this?"

"You can dig it up. I'm bringing the mike and the wire.

4

Tell your parents we're trying an experiment. And that's no lie."

Hobey grinned and Vance went on, "You're visiting me on January 4th, remember. And I'm visiting you. Is that clear to your embryo brain?"

"Dad's likely to ask where. He's a lawyer, don't forget."

"Where would you be visiting me?" Vance demanded scornfully. "You're like a centipede with cold feet. We'll sleep at Alcibiades' joint."

"Might as well be fired for a good reason as bad."

"How can they fire us? It'll still be vacation. Look, don't you want to go through with it?"

"Sure, but it's a good thing Master Ike's three thousand miles away. Alcibiades is a fighting word with him. You know what he said."

*   *   *   *   *

Colton Muir and his roommate, Steve Livey of Idaho, headed for the Hall, bags in hand. Colt made his home with the MacQuarrie family, and Steve had been invited to spend the holiday on their farm.

They made a noticeable pair. The tall, sandy-haired Scot was nineteen, two years older than his fellow-juniors at Ironwood. He gave the impression of hard-packed flesh on strong bones. Steve was eighteen and had the bowlegged gait common to those who lived astride a horse. He was also light but wind-tanned with watchful blue-gray eyes.

Both young men were somewhat withdrawn from the vacation hullaballoo. Colt's eagerness to enter Cornell had kept his nose in his books so whole-mindedly that Neil Mac-

Quarrie said he was a disgrace to the dorm. Steve had just been sent to Ironwood by a grateful rancher for reasons Steve was modestly saying nothing about. He was finding the going hard. "Always loaded to the hocks with homework," was the way he put it. In each of them a personal dignity commanded respect for their way of life, but popularity passed them by.

As they neared the door of Headmaster Isaac Ironwood's office, Acting Headmaster Hartnung happened to come out. He said "Merry Christmas" to them both, and when Colt said, "Same to you, sir," the middle-aged man smiled and said, "If you mean that, thanks."

"Why shouldn't I mean it?" Colt replied with a grin, as he scanned the character in esteemed Master Harty's face for a clue to his meaning. The man was lined with firebrick, as Neil MacQuarrie had once said, but it certainly did not show.

"Mind stepping in a minute?" Harty asked, and to Steve, "I won't keep him four minutes."

The headmaster's office was large and sunny and looked unlike the torture-chamber that wrong-doers who had visited it, proclaimed. Isaac Ironwood IV, great-grandson of the school's founder, who was both owner and headmaster but now sojourning in England on a sabbatical leave he had given himself, had made this room a powerhouse of quiet enforcement of policy. In his dean of admissions, Harty, Headmaster Ike had left a better than competent substitute to reign in his stead. Colt had already found Harty a stanch friend who had taken a personal interest in his progress. Harty had even abated rules to enable Colt to pursue chemistry instead of sports in the afternoons.

Harty drew a chair for Colt near his and said, "I want

to ask a favor. I take you into my confidence, Colt, because you're older than the others and because I trust you."

Colt had learned to say nothing when he had no clue as to what to say. He felt sure that the favor must be difficult if it called for so much introduction from this man of few words.

"You can appreciate that I want to hand this school back to Headmaster Ike next June in good condition. You probably are aware of certain undercurrents that are wearing away the morale of the student body. You also know that boys are delightfully indifferent to trouble until it hits them in the stomach."

Colt's own background had taught him to keep his face idle and his mind busy. So he showed none of his disturbing inability to get Harty's drift.

"I intend to move heaven and earth to rectify this condition." Harty's jaw jutted a little. "And you can help me immeasurably by one small move on your part."

"I'd like to repay your kindness," Colt said quietly.

"I believe you're sincere in that and will show you how it can be done."

Colt felt the warmth of irritation invading him. He had let Harty skirmish around and already he was in a vulnerable position.

"Last May, a bunch of willful young politicians got Bill Ordley elected Student Body President," Harty went on. "This made a bad dent in the democratic principle. But Master Ike is so sold on democracy, that he puts up with such mistakes, in order that the school may learn better. He apologized to me, I may say in confidence, for leaving me with this

7

weak spot in the setup. I want to steer the school back into the true course by electing a S.B.P. next May who is strong enough to repair the damage and forestall further damage. I've had my eye on your class, Colt, and see no one so able to do both things as yourself."

So that was it! Colt was angry—and in a tough spot. The duties of the S.B.P. were many and continuous. He was angry because Harty knew that he must devote his time and energy to his studies. On the other hand, Harty had given him the scholarship that made Ironwood possible. The man must be in a jam to make this request.

Colt had been in a squeeze before and sparred for time. "You'd better choose someone you can elect," he said tightly.

"We of the faculty do no electing," Harty said gravely. "Please be clear about that. Master Ike lays down a rule of hands off. So I'm talking to you as man to man, not as master to student, and only because I know you appreciate Ironwood. You believe me?"

Colt felt a surge of affection and respect for this man who met you on the level. "I believe you, but I don't think you realize how little chance I'd have of getting the vote."

"Naturally I've weighed the chances." Harty rose, as if Colt had agreed and Colt felt the unwelcome warmth returning. "You have to take certain steps, of course. The first is to move downstairs. No S.B.P. has ever been elected from the third floor dorm. The seniors don't get to know him."

"I'd hate to leave Steve Livey."

"Bring him with you. The next step ought to be easier. Circulate a bit, Colt. Attend the Turnabout Dance in January."

"You're the second person to suggest that," Colt said with a grin. Harty burst into laughter. "I suppose you put Ellen up to it," Colt accused him.

Harty laughed louder. "No, you suspicious something-or-other. Ellen Waring doesn't need to be prompted. I suppose you told her you had to work."

Colt did not mind being teased about *this* girl. "I told her I couldn't dance," he said.

"Then she told you that she didn't care much about it, either."

Colt's grin widened. "Do you listen in on every conversation?"

"No, but I know something about women. Now, this is an order: visit us a couple of times during vacation. My wife's expert in the kind of shuffling they call dancing at the moment. She'll coach you sufficiently for you to take Ellen Waring out on the floor and give her a valuable surprise. All girls love to dance—with the right man. How's that?"

It fitted in so happily with what Colt really wanted that he could only say, "I obey orders. Thanks."

Harty's hand was on the doorknob. "You and I are now conspirators, Colt. Honest ones, but under the necessity of secrecy. If you decide to help Ironwood and me, don't tell *any*body, except Steve, who is admirably close-mouthed. Above all, don't give anyone the impression that you want the Student Body Presidency."

"Is that irony? Master Cecil's trying to drill irony into Sid Dalton and me."

"That's another matter I'd like to talk over with you, Colt,—when you decide." Harty's smile had vanished.

Colt knew he hadn't a chance when this man wanted something badly. "You clinched it when you threw in Mrs. Harty."

"You mean you will join hands with me?" The relief in Harty's voice moved Colt strangely.

"I'll be Johnny-on-the-job, Master Harty."

"Remember the day Neil MacQuarrie brought you to see me?"

"I ought to. It changed my life."

"I sized you up then as a man to tie to in an emergency. Now I'm sure of it."

They shook hands and Colt left. He was aware that his promise was going to shove him aside from his determined course, and the Scot in him rebelled. But he had been taught to pay his debts, and he clearly owed Harty this—and Mrs. Harty, too, if she could teach his dumb feet.

* * * * *

The bell rang for lunch for those delayed by train or plane connections. Neil MacQuarrie was waiting impatiently for the family car, and his roommate, Scupper Riley, was keeping him company. They were both brash tenth-graders, and were now amusing themselves by trying to get the goat of Bill Ordley, the unrevered Student Body President.

Scupper was sure that Ordley fancied himself in his swagger overcoat and called out, "Whose body did you take that off of, Bill?" This was a gibe at Ordley's illicit poker game, which Scupper held should be listed along with Latin in the school catalogue, it was so educational.

"Seen Lucille?" Ordley had the ill-sense to ask.

"She just left with Sid," Neil lied. "Too bad, Bill."

"You know the difference between you and a real bad man, Bill?" Scupper asked with a leer. "He's got a price on his head, but you've got it in your pocket." This jab referred to the not-too-hidden fact that Bill had bought his election.

Neil laughed louder than the jest warranted and Bill withdrew from the porch, after an unprintable snarl, to look for Lucille. Sid Dalton soon appeared with four suitcases and four girls. He was a genial giant, six feet two, whose family hoped would enter Princeton, but who intended to major in the Olympics.

Scupper was a respecter of importance, and while he had to continue kidding or expire, his tone changed at once. "You pass Bill Ordley, Sid? Neil here told him that you'd gone off with Lucille and ten other girls, but you've got only four!"

The four burst into a rainbow of titters, and Sid said, "Lucille's safe, I reckon. Teacher Minnie's giving her some advice."

The laughter that this picture brought on was interrupted by a furious barking from the car driving up. Scupper recognized the hairy head of Neil's beloved mongrel and said to his roommate, "One of the two muzzles I'm giving you for Christmas is for Bear."

"What a coincidence!" Neil retorted. "It's just what I picked out for you—after deciding against rat-poison."

Bear ended this exchange by tackling Neil low. The boys greeted Mr. Robert MacQuarrie as Ian MacQuarrie, Steve, and Colt appeared. Ian said at once to Neil, "There's no room in the car for that noise."

"I didn't bring him. He followed," Mr. MacQuarrie

said. "Neil, you and Bear up front with me," he added with the quiet air of a man used to solving difficulties. "The rest of you tuck in in back."

Colt was finishing stuffing their bags in the rear, when a grizzled man thrust his head through the car window and said, "Merry Christmas to you all. But if you boys break training, I'll sell your skins to a baseball factory." George Kress's searching gray eyes barely permitted a twinkle to be seen.

"Same to you, Coach."

"Be good, yourself."

"Merry Christmas."

When the car was out of hearing Ian said, "They don't come better. He's the cornerstone of this school."

2 -
Vance's Hearing-Aid

Vance, as usual, was wishing that Hobey would hurry. The tunnel was so hot that sweat trickled down his spine. The headphone pinched. The least movement stirred up dust until the air was thick enough to eat. If he turned off the flashlight to save the battery, the darkness filled up with spiders, rats, and things.

All Hobey had to do was follow the wire they had laid along the tunnel to the cellar under the Green Room, sneak out and around and in through the Conservatory to the organ in the Green Room, turn on the mike and ask Vance if he could hear. At the longest it should take him five minutes and he'd been gone fifteen. He must have been spotted by night watchman Bagley, or Miss Kailer in the office. Hobey was not a lucky guy.

So far Vance's usual luck had done for both. They had stopped first at Alcibiades' joint over in the Village, engaged a bed for the night, changed into work clothes, reached the school at dusk when Miss Kailer would be eating in the kitchen cafeteria. They had finished up the wiring job, prepared for by weeks of planning and secret application at night, between Bags's punctual rounds.

Hobey, of course, had neglected to bring the white mouse, or a sub. So Vance had sewed a silk thread to an old baseball and rolled it beneath the floor from the organ to the vent in the Conservatory. He had plenty of imagination underneath his dead-pan exterior. His high-strung nature pressed to get the thing in hand done. "Do be patient, dear," his mother was always saying. "Nonsense!" his father would contradict. "It's steam that pushes you out ahead. Don't stop the boy."

At home Vance had practiced pulling the wool over his mother's eyes. He continued the practice at school. It gave you a feeling of power to do as you wanted, and more power when you got others to do as you wanted. Power was his own discovery, and he kept it to himself. Even as a tenth grader he had tasted power in helping Bill Ordley into office. Now with this hearing-aid, as he called the listening apparatus, he would learn what was on the faculty's minds. Real power. If only Hobey hadn't been caught! Vance began calling his roommate names of dazzling directness. In the middle of an elaborate insult, he jumped as a thunderous "Can you hear me?" smote his eardrums.

"Not so loud, you fool!" Vance snapped.

"Come up, quick," Hobey was urging. "I've found pay dirt."

Vance couldn't ask what in thunder he meant. He hid his headphone by the other behind a pipe and started out. It worked. It really worked. He felt the same big lift that had come to him at Thanksgiving when the listening-post idea hit. Funny Maxton's riding of Sid Dalton had struck the spark. Vance's imagination had pictured himself restoring justice and getting a whale of a kick out of the process. If it was right for people to have an underground in wartime for the sake of justice why wasn't it virtuous to start one in school where so much injustice flourished—in English V b, anyway.

The Green Room, where Hobey should have been waiting, was dark and empty. Vance noticed a pencil of light in Headmaster Ike's private office. He tiptoed over and found Hobey playing his safe-breaker flash on a large oblong container, a card file.

"Hear me all right?" Hobey whispered.

"You ruined my eardrums. Why yell?"

"I didn't yell. I didn't talk much louder than this. It must be a good connection. Boy, we'll be able to hear Teacher Minnie scratch her head with that pencil!" Hobey held up a card. "Look what I found. Ike's file. He's got each one of us downgraded to the bone. It beats the F.B.I."

"You've got a heck of a nerve," Vance said.

"You going righteous on me?" Hobey exclaimed, for he was incapable of Vance's subtle distinctions. "What's the diff between listening in on the faculty and looking at their old cards?"

"If you don't know, I can't tell you."

"Then I'm going on with it."

"No you're not," Vance said. "The hearing-aid's a sporting proposition. Rifling a guy's private desk is something else. Put the darn thing back and let's go. It's almost nine and time for Bagley."

"Bags won't come. It's vacation."

"Put it back, I tell you," Vance commanded. "We're taking no chances on ruining the whole thing."

"Don't you want a look at yourself?" Hobey held out a card. "Ike's got you down cold, all sorts of dope. Take a squint at your progress chart, as he calls it. You'll be surprised."

"Where in blazes did you dig up this file?" Vance asked.

"It was out on the desk. Maybe Harty was working on it."

"Well, stick those cards back and fix everything just as you found it. I'll stand at the door in case Bags is on the job. Make it snappy."

"Look, Vance, I've picked out the guys and girls we ought to know more about. Why can't I take them over to Alcibiades' tonight? I've got some girls I wouldn't mind dating. Boy, can you imagine . . ."

"Start putting those cards back, or I'll shove your mangled body under Diane's bed as a souvenir."

Hobey bowed to Vance's leadership and said, "Hold the light for me." In the silence both became conscious of a patter of clicking sounds on the polished floor of the Green Room.

Vance killed the light and they stood in the eerie darkness, listening. The sounds pattered nearer, and Vance whispered into Hobey's ear, "It's Blackie. Let's sit down on the floor. Sshh."

They subsided to the floor, sitting close together behind the desk. This was serious. To be caught looting a private file of such confidential information could be grounds for dismissal, and both boys knew it. For Bagley would surely be following Blackie, his moth-eaten Scottie and nocturnal companion, trained to a silence as complete as the watchman's own. Then Vance realized with a sinking stomach that he had left the door into Ike's office open—a dead giveaway.

The two malefactors sat as still as the furniture. The click-clicks were in the room, coming towards them. Vance felt the invisible weight of Blackie's bulk and the cold wet nose kissing his face and neck in the joy of reunion, though without even a whimper of delight. Vance gently lifted Blackie so that he faced the doorway and gave his rump a shove. The dog merely wheeled and came back for more.

The ray from Bagley's lantern caught the office ceiling and crept downward. "What you doin' in there, Blackie?" came the flat disinterested voice. "Come along, boy."

Blackie was pulled, torn between habitual obedience, and his love of the warm-smelling animals who usually ran on their hind legs. They fed him ice-cream cone ends, hard cider, cokes, or even the delicious carrion called hoagies. They never sat quiet like this, and rarely tried to push him away. Vance's noiseless assists in the direction of his master's voice were puzzling.

"What you into now, boy?" called Bags and started towards the desk. Vance gave the dog a hoist, and Blackie took the hint. They heard the claw-clicks departing and the old man say, "I know you're lonely, boy, but they'll be back tomorrow. Come along now." For a paralyzing instant the beam of the dark lantern flashed over the room above desk level. Then the footsteps followed the click-clicks and died away.

"His mind's not on his work," Vance said with a relieved sigh. "I've a notion to report him."

17

Hobey had no reputation for bravado to uphold. "I thought it was all up. I guess I wouldn't make a good second-story man."

Vance snickered.

*   *   *   *   *

They woke refreshed about ten the next morning, dressed, and found their way down to the small curtained room where Alcibiades' younger brother, Nestor, brought them a slovenly breakfast. The older Greek had not appeared. His business was largely nocturnal, like other prowlers. The place did not look romantic in the January morning light. Yet it was a magnet for the super-adventurous older boys at the school on the hill. Here, it was reputed, you could see life at close range if you stayed long enough.

"He be here soon," Nestor said. "Why you no come in car like other parents?"

Hobey laughed. "We're not parents, yet."

"Why you no come in car with parents?" the young Greek repeated tonelessly.

"They poor. Parents poor," Vance said to establish a point.

"No money," the Greek nodded. "We poor, too."

"You're poor all right," Vance said. "You've got a Ford truck and a Lincoln sedan and a TV and a nice house besides this hutch, and Alcibiades goes to Florida. That's poverty."

Nestor's olive face was expressionless. "He go to make business."

Vance nodded. "Rum comes from Cuba. Florida runs a long coastline. We know."

Alcibiades had entered as quietly as the weasel he re-sembled. He could be any age, Vance thought, maybe forty. He looked as if he had slept little and had overheard Vance. "Talk what you know," he ordered crossly. Nestor vanished.

"You'll like this," Vance said undaunted, for he was not one to shun a fight of wits. "We're here to talk what *you* know—money. We've got a market for your stuff up at the school. Candy, cokes, cards, funnies, smokes, you know, all the stuff. We've got a plan to run it in. There are 151 boys and 149 girls in the high school, and about 50 kids in the sub-school. That's 350 buyers. They all get good allowances. They'd spend one, two, five, maybe even ten bucks a month, if the stuff they want is offered them. There's six months to go. Say that adds up to four or five thousand bucks. How much of it do we get for setting up this market for you and your brother?"

Hobey was watching the Greek's face as Vance put on his sales talk. It was really evil when you got a close-up of it. The unwinking look scared Hobey who wasn't evil, but sim-ply a boy on a shaky foundation. Vance's face grew harder as he tried to out-sharp the Greek.

Then Hobey remembered the remark on his own file-card, "Tends to be Draper's toy." That had sobered him for a minute. And now, for a second minute, he tried to figure the cost to himself of their alliance in mischief that constantly grew more serious.

"Tell me this Nicky Dorritt?" Alcibiades was saying.

"He smart," Vance was adopting his talk to suit the Greek's range. "He never hangs around with us two. He never gets caught with the weed. He can talk clean when he

19

has to. In a Sunday School they'd pick him to pass the hymn-books. He's got that kind of a face. But his thinker, O *bro*ther!"

"Yes, yes, but how he not get caught with the cigarettes?"

"He gets over here free on Monday nights. Nicky's poor, so he picks up the shoes that need repairing, takes them to Toglio next door, and picks up the mended bunch to take back. See? He'll stop in here for your package, and bring it with the shoes. He'll leave it where I'm to get it, and I do the rest. See? Simple as supper."

"The money? How do I get my money?"

"Nicky leaves that the next Monday."

"No good, no good. Too long."

"Why you old horse," Vance laughed. "Is one week too long to wait for a sure thing? Something better than $200 a month?"

"Too long," the Greek repeated.

Hobey was discouraged. It was easier asking your family for a bigger allowance. Vance didn't seem discouraged, though. Hobey had to admire Vance's patience. He could work himself up into the fanciest vocabulary on the dorm simply over cleaning up for Friday inspection, or doing the extra reading that Funny Maxton laid down in a voice like a ball-bat cracking 'em out. But when it came to something he had set his heart on, Vance could sit it out with anyone like a cat at a rat hole.

As the horse-trading continued, Hobey decided that he was not Vance's toy. He might be his pupil and accomplice as he was often his beneficiary. Besides, wasn't Vance going to make him Student Body President? In spite of the fact that

Vance didn't approve of the car that Hobey's parents had promised if he was elected. Vance was a funny guy. Here he was trying to get the best of Ironwood School, yet thought the promise of the car wrong. "If you can't see it, I couldn't tell you," Vance said and wouldn't explain. It was as crazy as setting up the hearing-aid and refusing to look at the file-cards.

The two voices drew Hobey back from his reverie. Then suddenly it was over. Alcibiades let a half-smile show and said, "I do." He left the room, Vance wiped his forehead and said, "Whew! The deal's on. You probably heard me guarantee the old snake $200 worth of business a month."

Alcibiades returned with three glasses of beer with the bubbles rising and winking. "You like nice drink? On me?"

Hobey thanked their host, but Vance pushed his arm back.

"Nix on that," he said to Hobey, and to Alcibiades, "We athletes are on a milk diet, didn't you know?"

Alcibiades was puzzled. "Why you go such a place?"

"Because it's more fun than a barrel of snakes. Also it's necessary, if you're going to be President of the United States. Come on, Hobe. We've got to pack our work clothes."

Toy or not, he was going to stick with Vance to the death, Hobey told himself. First, he was one heck of a good business man, a clown, and offered a new adventure every hour.

"I thought of a couple of things while that pickpocket was trying to snitch all the profits," Vance said. "One, we mustn't be seen going back together. I'll go first and register innocence. You won't like the other idea, but if you're going to make S.B.P., you oughtn't to go around with me any more."

Hobey was stunned. "You mean no more fun?"

"What's more fun than getting what you want? You want that sports car, don't you? It's not going to be a cinch. Council nominates two candidates, don't forget. That's the catch. It might be Bellman, and I think he can be licked, but it's also likely to be Colt."

"Never," Hobey exclaimed. "I wish Council *would* put him up. He wouldn't get ten votes."

"I'm taking no chances. If you want that car *sure,* play safe. Don't forget that when it comes to S.B.P., it's respect that counts, not popularity."

"Yeah, they respect Bill Ordley!" Hobey hooted.

"It took our hard work and a great big fluke to put him in, and then only by four votes. Do you want to play?"

Hobey hesitated. Divorce from Vance was a dreary price. No midnight counsels, no crumming expeditions to Alcibiades, no help with math, no . . .

"We'd still see as much of each other as we wanted," Vance offered, "only not in public. You'd better ask for a room on the third floor. You could hint that you've reformed and might find it easier to reform with another roommate."

"You trying to can me?" Hobey flared up. "You know nobody has ever been elected S.B.P. from the third."

"I want you where you can do the most good," Vance replied reasonably. "This will draw more useful attention to you than anything you can do. Now, think it over. I've got to be going. You come in about twenty minutes."

22

3 -

Turnabout's Fair Play

At boys' end, the second floor dorm housed the seniors and most of the juniors. The proctor's desk stood opposite the stairway, and because Thursday night was the usual time for faculty meeting, faculty members were at a premium for the combination policing-and-tutoring job that went on at this desk.

As this was the first faculty meeting since the hearing-aid had been set up, both Vance and Hobey were wild to listen in. So Vance dropped a word in Student Body President Bill Ordley's ear. Ordley had no idea *why* his chief backers wished to absent themselves illegally from their room during study hour, but he had learned long ago not to ask questions. All he did, at Vance's instigation, was to relieve his next in authority, Andrew Bellman, at the desk. Bellman's intellectual eyebrows rose, but he reserved *his* questions for his instructors, and gladly went to his room.

Consequently, when Vance and Hobey in quick succession asked permission of Ordley to visit the lav, Ordley need only nod. Six minutes later, Vance and Hobey had donned headphones and were actually present at a faculty meeting. A confused murmur of voices indicated that Acting Headmaster Harty had not yet called the meeting to order. They identified Harty's firm tones, and supposed him close to the mike, for Harty and dean of boys Henry Vanner were conversing in undertones. Yet their words were easily picked up. The eavesdroppers gathered that rooming arrangements were being discussed, and suddenly Hobey thrilled to hear his own name. Henry Vanner said, "It looks to me as if Hobey Tyler has turned over a new leaf."

"I'm afraid it's not so simple," came Harty's voice. "Nothing in the dorms is as it looks, as you will someday be convinced."

"Why should he ask to leave Vance Draper? He told me that his parents wished him to work harder."

"I wish his parents had that much sense," Harty remarked.

Hobey felt Vance's elbow in his ribs and burst out, "I'll tell them that, the goon!"

"You will *not!*" Vance retorted. "Are you nuts? Not one thing we hear down here is ever to be repeated. Get that, or I'll tear the thing out. Now listen."

"Their motives are not often complex," Harty was saying. "Eat, drink, and be merry, or cheese it, the cops! But that doesn't mean they are simple to come at. Hobey's parents have always wanted him to work harder. It's chronic with them, and I doubt that Hobey has got suddenly supersensitive about it. I do know that it's necessary to look under the new leaf for the real reason. Meanwhile, we can accept the

24

move as a godsend, a break. But who're you putting in with Vance, Henry? It's the equivalent of throwing the baby to the wolves."

"There must be someone who's incorruptible," Henry Vanner said, almost wistfully. The boys laughed so that dust rose and choked them.

"Master Ike thinks there must be," Harty said with a laugh. "It's why he keeps Ironwood going."

"Well, there's Savery Miller," the dean of boys stated without too much conviction. "At least he doesn't smoke, won't crum over to the Greek's, won't do the other things. He's an admirable bundle of won'ts. I don't say he could reform Vance but I do think he wouldn't crumble."

"What if Savey objects to facing the wolves?" Harty asked. "He's all you say, and a lot more. But he lacks confidence."

"Couldn't you tell him that he is doing a service to the school by filling in with Vance? He idolizes Ironwood."

"I'm not sure I like that," Harty objected.

"Good old Harty!" Vance exclaimed admiringly. "I'm for that man."

"Even while you cut his throat," Hobey commented.

"A game's a game," Vance said impatiently. "Push that into your thick head. This is all a kind of poker, with big stakes, and Harty won't cheat. Listen."

Vanner was saying, "If Bud Tracy moves upstairs to room with Hobey, as I know he'd like to do, and if Savey moves in with Vance, then you've got the empty room on the second floor you wanted for Colt and Livey. It fits like a glove,

25

and we can't have Savey's reluctance interfere. Certainly you can apply a little pressure."

"I'm not sure that I'll need to," Harty said. "Leave that part of it to me, Henry. I'll keep you posted. I think that all the boys, Hobey, Savey, and Bud Tracy, can move on Sunday after Meeting."

"Get that?" Vance said to Hobey. "So Colt's to come down. You know what that means?"

"He and Steve are both juniors," Hobey retorted. He was always nettled when Vance underrated his intellect. "Why shouldn't they come down?"

"I think, and shoot me if I'm wrong, I think Colt reeks with concealed ambition, my child. I think he smells bait, the S.B.P."

"Do you want Bellman and Brick Evans and me to resign so he can have it? Brick and Andy and I all have a chance, but Colt hasn't a chance."

"Grow up," Vance said. "You aren't grown up until you've learned that nothing's impossible." He chuckled. "Savey and I as roommates! I bet you'd have said that was impossible last week. I can't wait till Sunday."

"What are you going to do to him?"

"You'll see," Vance said and then added roughly, "and keep your trap shut at the same time. I'm running this show and don't need Diane Ebbitts' help."

Hobey wanted to kick Vance but didn't. He had found silence the most soothing reply to Vance in this slam-bang mood, when things were going his way and he wanted no interference. And it was true that Diane had a way of worming secrets out of him. Just the way she said Ho—bey. . . .

26

A gavel rapping recalled Hobey's wandering thoughts to the faculty. "Before we bend our necks to the yoke," Harty said with schoolmaster jocularity, "Miss Linbright tells me that Diane Ebbitts' card is missing from the confidential file. I am suspected, for I had the file out the night before school resumed, and was called home and left it out for an hour or so. But I was not *that* interested in Diane. Will someone clear me by confessing that he or she has absent-mindedly abstracted the card? It is strictly against our rule, but this time the culprit will not be sent to the mines."

Hobey broke out into a sweat of apprehension. Silence in the Green Room was followed by murmurs.

"Well, we cannot wait," Harty broke in, with more than a suspicion of impatience. "If someone remembers, please leave the card on Master Ike's desk. I prefer mysteries between book covers. The card vanished. Now let us resume study of the schedule."

Vance lifted Hobey's headset off and said, "We'd better go now. You didn't take Diane's card, did you?"

"I didn't mean to. I'd slipped it into my pocket for special attention and forgot. It's in my bureau, under the shirts."

Vance was tempted to blow his partner to bits. "I think you underrate life, just a little bit, Hobe," he said with deceptive gentleness. "I know the head on your shoulders is usually Diane's, but it isn't enough. If Harty ever backtracks to you for this, you won't be S.B.P. in May. For you won't be here. And I won't either. So do you mind if I take a hand?"

"What can you do?" Hobey asked.

"Tonight, when you're asleep and Bags has passed by, I'll wipe the card free of fingerprints, just in case, and drop it on Ike's desk, and Harty'll think someone has been afraid to own up and sneaked back with it, and that will be that. I do hope Bud Tracy knows how to look after you."

*　　*　　*　　*　　*

Once a month the Alumni Gymnasium, as Master Ike liked it called, was the scene of a leap-yearish sort of dance where the girls invited the boys, and where, in theory at least, there were no wall-flowers.

On this January evening, the Decorating Committee had outdone previous committees by rigging up a moon that shone and hiring a live orchestra from Trenton. The musicians were instructed to import some atmosphere from the South Seas. They complied, by means of languid moans and seductive rhythms, so that even the non-dancers questioned their abstemiousness.

The faculty members who took turns being present to see that the two inches of air-space between partners was more or less observed, were enjoying the happy change from the din of the twice-a-week dances. The moonlight also lightened their duties of inspection; they couldn't see. Word of this happy novelty had attracted even hardened abstainers. Savey Miller stood by the main entrance as inconspicuously as he could and still be present. He felt the silent anguish of non-participation with greater pain than usual.

Savey's case was hard to figure out. Although his growth had been slow, he had lengthened out into an attractive boy. But his were the virtues not in demand on the dance floor. His tastes were intellectual, his habits beyond reproach.

Nor was he popular in the dorm. Beer could not tempt

him for he had never tasted it. He knew nothing about poker, had never played hall hockey at 1 a.m., or talked cars, or gone crumming to the Greek's, or been invited to a bull session of the Midnight Club. His speech was limited to words that could be printed, and his shyness with girls was all but total.

Yet Savey was in love and more in love than were most of the daters on the happily dimmed floor. Fortunately Lola Wilson was not present to add to his chagrin and loneliness. The young woman, had proven too attractive at her task of assisting Jane Dickson in the Library. Since she needed the job and did not enjoy repulsing over-friendly seniors, she ignored the dance. The boys, unfortunately, understood this. Savey rebelled at the injustice when he heard them call this charming girl with the warm-blooded smile "Little Iceberg." He felt sure it was libel. He did not know enough to recognize it as an invitation to warm up a little.

Savey heard voices. Neil MacQuarrie and Scupper Riley had left the ping-pong table in the gameroom to enjoy their usual sport of characterizing the poor lugs who called hauling a skirt around the floor, fun. Yet a faint doubt of their own judgment had begun to blunt their wit. Could so many otherwise sane fellows be wrong?

"Look at that little wootz Pesky's hooked with?" Scupper pointed out.

Neil's attention was on another couple. "Why the slink! Colt swore he couldn't dance, and look at him!"

Scupper followed Neil's nod to a pair moving with ample grace—Colt and Ellen Waring. Neil did not laugh. Colt's treachery stabbed him. Colt's hanging out with the non-dancers had upheld Neil's scoffing at otherwise good guys who tied themselves up for a whole evening with one date. Now Colt had fallen and Neil knew that he would have to go with the tide.

At this moment he caught sight of Savey in the shade of a moonlit palm. The boy's eyes, Neil noticed for the first time, were alive and beautiful. He must now admit that Savey was human after all, for he followed Savey's glance and saw Lola Wilson approaching him, heard her invite Savey to dance, watched with amazement as Savey led her out onto the luminous floor, and actually put his arm about her, minding the two inch rule, of course, but moving happily away with a look on his face that somehow made him a man.

"Look who Savey's copped!" Scupper exclaimed. "I wouldn't mind cutting in myself."

This from the Scupper! A night of treasons. Neil retorted, "Only girls can cut in, you dope. And who will?"

Savey felt secure from interruption for the same reason and was happy. "You dance so well, Savery," Lola was saying, although her toes were somewhat bruised.

"Anyone could dance well with you," Savey admitted, and his longing to call her Lola instead of the correct Teacher Lola increased.

"Thank you, I wish it were true," Lola replied. "I wonder why they heat this place so abominably. It must be ninety."

Savey was taken aback. "I hadn't noticed. I guess it is hot."

"Oh, look! Isn't that attractive?" Lola recklessly diverted Savey's attention from his dancing to the punch bowl, disguised as a coconut. "Might we?"

Savey gallantly acceded, for he was thirsty, too. He ladled out the grape-colored drink into glasses and Lola pointed out two chairs at some distance. "This is what I've been waiting for, *so* long, Savey. I never have a chance to talk with you. In the Library I must be so strict about silence."

"Nor I with you," Savey agreed, "There's so much I want to say."

"Really?" The girl could be charming. "About your writing?"

"Well, partly." Savey was not thinking about his writing.

"Master Cecil says you have genuine talent."

"*Funny* does?" Savey colored. He had not meant to blurt out the name that Vance had pinned on Cecil Maxton in bitterness.

Lola ignored the break. "Of course he does. He showed me your theme about Mr. A. E. Skyprop. What do the initials stand for?"

They stood for *Alter Ego,* since Mr. Skyprop was a serious, and secret, creation of Savey's longing. Something lacking in Lola's tone, a certain shallowness of interest, warned Savey to keep the truth about A. E. Skyprop to himself. "But Master Cecil gives me C's. Colt gets B's and even B plus," Savey went on with a strange heat for him.

"Probably because Colt tries so hard," Lola said lamely.

"My hat! Don't I try?"

"Master Cecil says you've got the best ears and eyes of anyone here, and they're so important in writing. I think he gives you C's to stimulate you to still better work."

"An A would stimulate me a lot," Savey said.

Lola's voice lowered. "Can you keep a secret, Savey?

31

Hobey Tyler and Vance Draper are no longer going to room together, and Master Harty must choose a trustworthy boy to replace Hobey, for Vance is so very, so *very*—what shall I say? persuasive. Master Harty is paying you a high compliment. He's going to ask you to move in with Vance." Lola countered any possible objection by looking directly into Savey's eyes.

"Me?" Savey was too startled to go on.

"I know how you feel, Savey." Lola laid her hand gently on his wrist. "But you *can* do it."

"Vance'd throw me out of the window. I'd bore him to suicide."

Lola chose to laugh. "I can't see Vance suiciding. He's too fond of his own superior self."

"No, but seriously. I couldn't room with him, Teacher Lola." Savey did not even wish to call her Lola at the moment. He was beginning to piece things together, the dance, one turn about the room, then this—and a certain obtuseness about A. E. Skyprop.

"It would do you good," Lola almost blurted out, but did say, "It would do Vance so much good, Savey. You could help him, and I don't mean only with his English, which needs it." She tried the direct glance again. "You probably guess that that's why Master Harty is choosing you."

"I don't particularly want to do anybody good."

"Why Savey!" It was Lola's turn to be disillusioned.

"I don't *particularly* want to be good myself!" Savey added from his depths.

"Savey Miller, what's got into you?" Lola cried, then she remembered her promise to Master Harty. "You do love Ironwood School, don't you, Savey?"

"Everybody loves Ironwood School," he commented.

"That's not true. Lots of boys, and girls too, can't wait to be graduated from here."

Lola's eye had been on the dancers, and said with new zest, "Look who's coming," she whispered. "I do believe she has designs on you, Savey."

Savey saw a girl, a fellow-junior, named Cornelia Craig, heading their way. He had admired her mind from afar; but now it was eclipsed in a gauzy dress that removed her still farther. She was indeed lovely to look at, if you preferred blondes, and he remembered that she and Lola were congenial friends. "She's just coming to speak to you," Savey said.

Her look spoke differently. An invitation to dance was clear before she stopped before Savey. "May I cut in, Teacher Lola?" she said in as delightful a voice as he had ever heard.

"I'm sure I should be rude and not let you, if I didn't have to go," Lola said smoothly. "Savery, I've enjoyed this so much. Will you think over what we'd all like you to do— for Ironwood's sake?"

Savey was caught. He could hardly refuse in front of Cornelia, and nodded. "I've enjoyed it a lot, Teacher Lola."

Then, as Lola receded, he looked at the vision who had hardly ever noticed his presence and said, with a deepening voice, "You don't have to go through with it, Cornelia."

"Why, Savey! I don't know what you're talking about."

"Well, I'm not that dumb. You're Teacher Lola's best friend and would do anything for her. True or false?" He smiled a bit grimly out of his new-found manhood, and the girl's awareness of him made up for lost time.

"Don't be silly," she said convincingly. "Let's have it."

4 –
S. Dalton vs.
W. Shakespeare

Savey Miller woke scared. The promise made in the moonlight seemed monstrous in January's thin morning twilight. Then he remembered. He had been so mad at Lola's asking him to dance as a softening-up maneuver and her probable bribing of Cornelia to take him off her hands, that he had forgotten himself and let go some and enjoyed it—and so had Cornelia. He could tell.

He remembered something else. He had told Cornelia, after she had promised to keep it secret, that Vance had asked him to room with him. Instantly after this insane boast, Savey was almost paralyzed with remorse. It was in a way a lie, though Lola had told him of Master Harty breaking the news to Vance and Vance's comment, "That's a good idea."

Vance had said it sarcastically, of course. But it seemed unnecessary to tell Cornelia that. Vance was going along with Master Harty in order to conceal some devilish trick, as when Vance and Hobey had provided Lily Waters with reading material, by filling his room to the ceiling with newspapers.

But Savey could always remember the thrill he'd had from Cornelia's "Why, Savey! I think that's wonderful." She hadn't thought it funny at all.

So Savey knew he had to go through with it. He peered at his roommate below. Bud Tracy had been out crumming half the night and was dead to the world. He'd probably scream at the news. Bud, Lola had confided, was to room with Hobey on the third.

The breakfast bell shattered Bud's slumber. "Tell 'em to save it," he mumbled. "I'm not getting up today."

"Tomorrow Hobey'll have the pleasure of getting you down to breakfast," Savey said.

"Make sense or shut up."

"You start rooming with Hobey after Meeting."

Bud woke another fraction and muttered, "What's that?"

"I'm moving into Vance's room."

Bud opened his eyes, "*I said shut up or make sense.*"

Savey said for the ten thousandth time, "You'll be late, Bud." Then for the first time he obeyed another impulse. He pulled the bedclothes off Sanders Tracy. Then, delighted with himself, he escaped to take a shower.

*   *   *   *   *

After Meeting Savey knocked on the door of Room 21 with a knee as his hands were full of books. Vance opened the door matter-of-factly and said. "You're just in time, Save. I need your advice."

Savey's surprise was complete. He had not hoped for a welcome; no one in the dominant group had called him "Save"; and to have Vance ask his advice was a shock, however pleasant.

35

"Stack your stuff anywhere. I'll help you move the rest," Vance continued unbelievably. "Sid's in hot water up to his neck, and we've got to get him out of it."

Savey had just enough presence of mind to adjust to this novel situation as he'd had in waking up to Cornelia. Vance and he made three trips before he was installed. Vance had actually asked him whether he preferred the upper or lower bunk, and had given him the desk nearest the window. He had overcome Savey's hesitation by saying, "You need it, Save. You sure read a lot. Wait till I show you the lighting system Hobe and I rigged up in case you have to study after lights-out. You can read all night if you want to."

Savey's capacity for surprise was numbed by now. The school shut off the electricity at 10 P.M. and Savey invariably wanted to read on. Bolder students used flashlights for their purposes. Savey abominated flashlights, and observed rules— "the solid foundations on which Ironwood stands" as the dean of boys phrased it.

So now he enjoyed a satisfaction in the ample light that would enable him to benefit from Vance's rule-breaking without actually breaking the rule himself. Even Master Harty did not expect him to reform Vance overnight. At the same time, Savey was too honest not to perceive the fallacy in his satisfaction. If he read by Vance's illegality, he did share the guilt. What could he do? To refuse the light would estrange him and Vance at once. To ask Vance not to break the rule had a prudish holiness about it that couldn't accomplish anything, anyway.

While arranging his things, Savey had noticed that Vance, out of habit, had lifted a pack of cigarettes from his

36

pocket and quickly buried it again with a quick glance to see whether he had been observed.

Savey gave no sign, though Vance's act was more disturbing than the light. Isaac Ironwood the Fourth had inherited a discipline that he might modify, but only a little. He was no martinet, and minor infractions of discipline incurred modest penalties. But smoking, drinking, and improper conduct while dating, were punished severely. The bolder experimenters developed skill in secrecy, Vance's hand had acted automatically, but it required connivance of his mind to strike the match. Before doing so, which was equivalent to admitting Savey into the inner circle, Vance knew that he must see where Savey stood.

"I know you've got the good of Ironwood at heart, Save," he began. "I guess you think Hobey and I are black sheep,— or rams." Vance's smile was an invitation to deny this.

Savey was tempted to, for when Vance chose to be friendly he was indeed persuasive. But Savey said, "Master Harty tells us not to judge by appearance."

"He's right, as usual," Vance said quickly. "I appear irresponsible to him, and he judges by those appearances. It's not very consistent."

Savey thought that Harty had something more to go on but held his peace, and Vance continued, "I know I've hacked around a lot, Save, though I'm not entirely alone." Again that smile inviting Savey in. "In fact, I guess you're the only guy I know who doesn't bend the rules a bit."

Savey liked being called a "guy" by Vance and suddenly disliked being set apart from him by virtue. "It depends on what you want, doesn't it?" he asked.

Vance gazed at the serious-eyed innocent with a beginning of respect. "That's a good answer," he said thoughtfully. "It explains a lot. You ought to post the faculty on that point of view, Save."

"Wouldn't they say that that's what they're trying to do—make you want what's best?"

"But who knows?" Vance countered. "Even Master Harty isn't that good. He can't even *know* whether you're cold or needing sleep. So how can he know what you want in—in other things. They trot us to Meeting, but they can't savvy what we're thinking or wanting. Maybe that's just as well," and Vance laughed.

"I think they know in a general way—because we show them."

Vance pondered that. "Maybe, but it's very general."

"What is it you *do* want?" Savey asked with an intensity of interest that surprised him.

"Me?" Vance's dark eyes lit up. "Maybe even I don't know. I want an education, even if I don't show up on the Honor List. But I want an all-round one. When we escape from here, we're up against the big world where you have to know your stuff. You've got to spot what's going on or lose out. It comes down to people, when you figure it out. So I aim to know people, Save. All kinds, but the live ones for sure."

Savey was excited. Nobody had ever talked to him quite like this. "How?" he asked from a heart he had never dreamt of showing to Vance. "I've been here as long as you and I don't know anybody very well."

"How?" Vance had never been asked that question. "How do you breathe? It's like that. You go 'round with them. You . . . well, I guess that's it. You go 'round with them, don't stand off, chuck in with them. See? You've got to like them of course. That's the first thing, maybe. I just naturally like people and like to be with them. That's why we herd together for bull sessions. You'd be surprised what you get to know, even when guys think they're covering up."

"I've never been in one," Savey confessed.

"Hang around, fellow." Vance grinned. "You'll find yourself shooting the bull like the rest of us in no time."

"They mayn't want me hanging around," Savey said with a sense of relief in revealing his fear at last.

"Can the false modesty, Save," Vance spoke forcefully.

"It's not false. That's the way I feel."

"Then get over it. Fellows take a guy's view of himself—until it gets too funny, at least. Just be yourself."

"That's what I'm trying to be, and you don't think much of it."

Vance was stopped for a moment. "Doggone it, we're having a bull session now, in a small way, Save, and you're holding your own end up. That's all it is, having an end to hold up. I've never had six words with you till now, and you make me back myself up. That's good. Fellows respect that, see?

"Now look, this is your room as well as mine. So Hobe and Ordley and Bellman and the rest can't complain when they find you in it. And they're curious about you, too. They know you've got a whale of a lot of brains. So be yourself and get wise to yourself. The only thing is, don't talk outside. What you hear in here stays here. You understand that?"

Savey knew that this was a crucial instant in his life.

Vance was offering him a partnership with him and his kind, "the live ones"—but on pain of utter secrecy. A dim warning rose in his mind but Savey said to it, "It's not my fault I'm here," and then to Vance, "I understand, and I promise." Then he smiled. "It isn't as if I haven't had some practice in keeping quiet, rooming with Bud."

Just then the first bell rang for the midday meal. "What are you doing after dinner?" Vance asked. "I haven't told you yet what I need your advice on. Can you come back here?"

"Sure," Savey agreed, and with more eagerness than he would have thought possible an hour earlier. The door banged open and Ordley barged in. "What do you know!" he said excitedly, and then observed Savey and stopped.

"It's all right," Vance said. "Savey's as safe as I am."

"Colt Muir's just moved down to this floor, and Steve with him. Get it?"

"I predicted it," Vance said smoothly. "So what?"

"Well, it means . . . it's his bid for S.B.P."

"Fine. It pays to know who you're fighting, don't you think?"

"But . . . well, it changes everything."

"For the better."

Savey listened and marveled at Vance, the general of future armies.

*   *   *   *   *

After Sunday's midday meal, the week's best, as three hundred critics saw it, and which Scupper Riley called "the binge," Savey hurried back to Room 21. Absent-mindedly he knocked, heard a, "Come in," and went in feeling sheepish, for the boys didn't knock. Sid Dalton, the only occupant, sat

40

sprawled in several directions over a chair too small for his length.

Sid made no reference to Savey's silly knocking on his own door, for Sid was a master at accepting things as they were. He extended this attitude to friend and foe. It made him seem both friendly and aloof, almost as if he didn't care, although that was not true. But now Sid was there, at hand, in Savey's chair, and they might yet be on even terms. This was a day of miracles.

"Vance said he wanted to see me," Sid explained humbly.

"Me, too," Savey said. One thing in common.

"Vance is a busy man," Sid observed, as if it was all right for Vance to keep him waiting. "Coach wants me at two-thirty."

This would be about Sid's recent difficulties with Funny Maxton's English class. Savey wanted to communicate his sympathy but was unsure as to how this was done, man to man.

"I think Vance wants me to get tutored," Sid went on. "Coach is kind of up in the air about it."

"Would you let me tutor you, Sid?" Savey asked with a wild hope. To help Sid and curb Funny at the same time would be a double joy, and he could probably find time.

"That's mighty good of you, Savey. But it's been tried."

"You tried a lot of times before you broke the pole-vault record," Savey argued.

"I don't mind trying again," Sid said evenly. "I just don't like wasting your time. If Shakespeare knew he was going to be thrown at kids, I guess he'd have had people talk plainer, don't you think?"

Vance slammed in. "Ginny stopped me in the hall," he said, as if that made up for any lateness. "Sid, she was so sore about the way Funny lit into you that she says something has to be done about it. She and Diane and Edna and Celia and probably Lorna will take turns tutoring you. How's that? Pretty soft. I'm going to play dumb myself and get me some tutoresses. Save, how'd you like to go haywire, like Hamlet, and need female assistance? Have you got brains enough to be as dumb as Sid?"

"No good," Sid interrupted gently. "Martha wouldn't especially like it."

"Well, she can't tutor you. She's got to like it."

"And I don't," Sid added with more finality. "*Five* girls! I don't see it. I'd rather Savey tutored me, if anyone does. He's offered."

"You're a funny guy," Vance said to Sid. He was referring to the athlete's attitude towards girls. It was objective. Sid liked having them around. If they could comprehend big league ball, he enjoyed them as companions. But they insisted on adoring him. They were always scheming to get him away from others. They had no idea of what it was to stay in training. They couldn't comprehend that sports came first and everything else that interfered went out the window. "And it's lucky they can't," Vance told Sid astutely. "If you'd consult the Bard, you'd know that hell hath no fury like a woman scorned. And sixty women!"

Sid got up, "I've got to go to Coach's house now. You want to start in on me this evening, Savey?"

They arranged to meet after Vespers. Sid left, and Andy Bellman, the patrician, the true high-brow, second to Savey on the Honor List, but also the paradox of the junior class, in that he preferred low company, arrived. He was followed by Hobey, big-shouldered Bill Ordley, and lively, only moderately corruptible Bud Tracy. They were all talking at once, evidently in a lather of excitement.

"It's good!" Bellman kept repeating. "Come, Vance, you've got to hear it."

"Shut up! Hear *what?*" shouted Vance. "Not any more of you, I hope."

"It's his tape-recording of Funny last Friday. His class," Hobey explained.

"Something went screwy half way through, but what we got is swell," said Ordley, who, typically was already taking credit for Bellman's coup.

"It's pure nuts!" Tracy put in delightedly. "If only Harty could hear it, he'd blast Funny right out of this school."

"That's irony," Vance said. "A pity Sid isn't here."

"It mustn't be mentioned," Bellman cautioned, "or we'll follow Funny to a new address."

"Come," Hobey said impatiently to Vance. "Andy's set it up in that practice room the piano cracks use."

"I think you're crazy," Vance said. "But we'll come. Drop the books, Savey, and be educated."

Bellman quickly took his leader's cue and said, "You'll be missing the show of the year if you don't."

Savey felt the electricity of these free-wheelers, and was thrilled to be included, even though it was Vance's doing.

"We're not telling Colt, I gather," Vance said to Bellman.

"Good gosh, no!" Hobey answered. "Colt thinks Funny's right up with Shakespeare. They both come from Oxford."

"Stratford, you dope," Bellman objected.

"Funny said Oxford."

"*He's* from Oxford, Shakespeare's from Stratford."

"Well, they must have a lot of wind over there," Hobey said.

"The girls mustn't find out, either," Tracy remarked.

"Sad but wise," Vance admitted. "I'd love to hear Ginny laugh. But if the faculty got wise to Andy's rigging up an ear-witness to their braying, they'd never know a minute's peace till we were fired."

"That's called playing with fire," Bellman said, for he had a childish delight in puns. The others did not bother to groan.

Sunday afternoon was a good time to do anything that was better unobserved. Some of the boys studied, some slept, some crummed over to the Village for amusements of questionable value. When the six entered the practice room, Bellman who owned the tape-recorder said, "Did any of you fellows know you were being taped Friday?"

Nobody spoke. "Why didn't Funny catch on? He's so smart," Tracy asked.

"One thing at a time is his motto," Vance remarked and the rest howled at the irony implied.

"I hid the recorder in the closet," Bellman explained. "I sat the mike on a cushion, to stop vibration, and Funny's clear English accent did the rest. Funny missed it because he can't see the obvious. If he could, he's stop riding Sid. He'd see that Sid's simply not cut out to be a Shakespeare authority."

"That's the trouble with these faculty cranks," Hobey said. "They want us to throw ourselves overboard and be like them. To the Hot Place with it."

"It's possible to live without being just like Funny," Savey ventured. Everbody laughed, rather indulgently.

"Get on with it," Ordley said. "We all know about Funny."

Bellman started the playback. "This is zero hour minus one," sprang at them in crisply clipped syllables. The boys roared with laughter in recognition of that voice.

"Shut up!" Vance ordered. "Save it, for cripes sake!"

". . . a review, today. On Monday, a test."

A subdued groan shuddered from the tape, and Savey tingled with excitement. Could this be Ironwood School!

"Bellman," the voice commanded, "all through our study of *Julius Caesar* I have been stressing what particular aspect?"

"Its tie-in with today," they heard Bellman say confidently.

"Right. Tyler, give a major instance of this tie-in, as you please to call it."

Hobey audibly cleared his throat. "You mean killing Caesar?"

"People are always being killed. What was there in Caesar's death that reminds us of today?"

"Caesar was a dictator, like Hitler, Stalin, and the rest."

"A superficial likeness. What's the deeper allusion, Draper?"

45

"I don't know anything deeper than death," Vance replied.

"Red herrying," Funny snapped. "To what do I refer, Miller?"

"The spiritual weakness of our so-called strong men," Savey said, and the listening Savey thrilled at the man-quality of the voice given to him by the tape.

"Exactly. Change a few names and this play is a mirror of modern times. Do you see the value of literature? It could have shown Mussolini and Hitler the underlying and unassailable truths of life and human nature, if they had had intelligences trained to understand. Now, Tracy, let's have another parallel."

Silence. Then the voice, slightly acid, said, "Girls to the rescue. Diane Ebbitts?"

"I'm not sure, sir."

"Edna Hallett."

"You mean the assassination?"

"I'm asking the questions. Lorna Weldon?"

"The irony in *Julius Caesar* matches the irony of politics today."

"Right. It's disheartening—and ominous, I might add—to have to hunt over so much territory for that answer. Ordley, kindly give me an instance of irony in the play."

Savey's tingle increased as the tape reminded him of Funny's growing chill and the debacle soon to burst on them. The tape's silence indicated that Ordley was thinking, and finally he said, "I hope you want me to say Mark Antony's funeral oration."

"It will do. And now, Dalton, an easy one for you, since

it mustn't be thought that I haven't the good of the basketball varsity at heart. Kindly furnish me with the gist, the key to Antony's great effort. Why do we call it ironical?"

The tape indicated the literary vacuum in Sid's handsome head. Savey shivered again as he had in class for Sid's sake.

Funny broke the silence with "Don't think, Dalton, if the effort is too painful. Simply recall my words heard to the point of tedium in this room. By the way, what, once more, is irony?"

"It's when Caesar was killed in front of Pompey's statue, sir."

Nobody laughed, for when Vance had perceived Funny's pleasure in his gibes, he decreed silence in retaliation. Even the girls in Vance's confidence had learned a facial control on a par with the dead pan of an American Indian. Funny wondered how they could be so dumb as not to see his jokes.

"Would it be irony if you fainted in front of Shakespeare's bust?" Funny was asking Sid.

"What's that got to do with it?" Sid said quietly, and the tape gave off a rustle of approval.

"Precisely my question," Funny said crisply. "I ask for bread and you give me a statue. I want a definition, Dalton, not an instance. I don't insist on anything original. Merely repeat what I have tried to pour so liberally into your head."

The tape paused, as if in expectancy, then Funny lashed out.

"I don't see how you do it, Dalton. What a marvel of concentration! How absolute your ability to evade every shred of instruction! You almost persuade me to become a scientist so that I could have the pleasure of dissecting your brain. It must antedate the Neanderthal. A primitive. The original cerebrum, perhaps. A thousand pities that you cannot cash in on this treasure now to a museum. You would never miss it."

"Horsefodder!" Vance was heard to whisper. "Listen to the beast!"

"I must forswear the scalpel, Dalton, but I shall not deny myself the pleasure of a nearer acquaintance. I foresee many fruitful hours with you and Shakespeare in conference. I hope a suitable substitute for you can be found for the basketball team . . ."

"You can't do that to him!" Hobey said aloud.

"I have the floor," Funny observed instantly. "And it is time that this was said, not only to you but to the school and its managers. This institution purports to be a school. At least that's the impression Headmaster Ironwood gave me in England. I repeat: it is a school, not a training camp for athletes. I propose to stop the mass irony of allowing parents to think that our marks refer to education, when they stand for the number of goals made in basketball or for your batting average in the national sport. Colton Muir, what is irony?"

"It's saying something that's the opposite of the literal meaning of the words. Or it's when something turns out just the opposite of an intention."

"Now I'm ready for an instance. Celia Nash."

"If the assassin's knife had turned and cut his own wrist."

"Excellent. A modern instance, Bellman."

"When a teacher's words boomerang on him, sir." A shout of cold laughter leaped from the tape. The boys listening roared back their approval in bellows of guffaws and drowned out the tape.

"Shut *up!* Listen, you fools!" Vance commanded, but even he could not stem that flood.

"Play it over," Hobey cried when the noise died away.

Bellman rewound and they listened again to that inspired, "When a teacher's words boomerang on him, sir." Then the laughs and Funny's equally able retort, "That's only when the words meet a solid substance—and bounce." A solid silence met his crack and they heard Tracy murmur, "Pause for applause." The class laughed again and Vance said, "Oh, what a fall was there, my countrymen!" The tape gave off the girls' appreciative shrieks, and they heard Funny say, "Don't forget, I have the last word, and it comes next Monday."

It was here that the recording clouded. Bellman stopped the tape, and Vance said, "I'd almost risk my stay here to play that off for Master Harty."

"Well, I wouldn't," Bellman cut in. "Irony's an active principle."

"Maybe Funny's right," Vance said. "Irony's what makes life go *ping!*"

"But what'll we do about Sid?" Bellman said.

"Savey's going to tutor him," Vance said.

"But he's got only the rest of today," Tracy objected.

"I could get him to memorize a lot of instances of irony and definitions," Savey said. "If he got those answers right, Funny would be astonished and maybe let him by."

"Be sure he learns Funny's pet instance—leading a horse to water and then the brute won't drink," Tracy said.

"My favorite illustration is Funny," Bellman said. "He's the capital *I* in irony, like a prize fighter who knocks himself out with his own haymaker."

They laughed. "The irony is that actually Funny's not a bad guy," Vance said, and Savey wished he had said it. "Coach bawls us out, too."

"Yes, but how?" Bellman countered. "He doesn't peel the skin off you, layer by layer, and salt the raw flesh. Kress doesn't sit back and admire his own wit, either. He's all for us winning."

"Well, one thing sure, don't let Sid know we're trying to ship Funny back to England. He'd crab the works," Vance said. And to this they all agreed.

5 -

Progress Behind
All Fronts

Colt and Steve Livey held their own bull sessions, usually after lights-out, and always so low-toned that even a master, pausing outside the door of Room 29, would not hear.

Colt wondered if blind luck or all-seeing Providence had brought them together. He had not thought much about roommates. Life had been chancy for so long, that he was used to taking what came. If the guy was half human and could understand that Colt had come to Ironwood with one idea: Cornell, he could make out.

When he reached the room assigned on that September day, Colt saw the rear side of some blue jeans, a much-washed flannel shirt, a black head peering out into the trees. The head turned, disclosing a tanned face, dark eyes, whose level look was as noncommital as an unopened letter. They exchanged names, shook hands—and resumed the quiet that was natural to them.

Colt was relieved that Steve was no spill-over at the mouth, no pestering kid, no rich boy. He was interested to find that Steve's jeans had sat long in a saddle as a working cowboy's chief garment. It was long, however, before Colt gathered that Steve was also an orphan and had made his own way from the age of twelve. It took still longer for Steve to divulge that a fellow-rancher, for whom the boy had done some great service, which Steve didn't go into, had offered him an education. By chance an ex-Ironwoodian heard and helped get him a scholarship.

"I reckon luck's riding on my shoulder," Steve said. "I don't aim to scare it off, neither."

"Wasn't it hard to leave that country?" Colt asked.

"Sure. Choosing between trails where they fork off is no fun. But I reckoned I could always go back to the hitch rack if this didn't pan."

They traded their pasts so gradually, that Steve, who never asked a personal question, would never have heard of Colt's earlier connection with a Brooklyn gang, the Hi-Gunners and how he had managed to find a new life, if Neil hadn't aired it all during Christmas Vacation.

"And they call the West wild!" was Steve's amused reaction. "Sounds like there's more gun-pulling in that bandit roost of yours than in all of Idaho. I used to tickle when an Easterner'd sidle up and ask me to point him out an outlaw. I see now, it was just so he could boast about New York's." The tall boy's eyes shone with the smile that so rarely reached his lips.

It was during Christmas vacation, too, that Steve was shown a photograph of Sandra Marquis by the mischievous Neil. "And you let her get away from you?" Steve exclaimed to Colt. "I'm ashamed of you, boy."

"She sent him a Christmas present from Paris," Neil said. "Her parents took her away to break up her engagement to a Navy boy. She and her brother are going to school in Switzerland."

For the first time Colt saw Steve laugh outright, right down to his heels. But he made no comment. Steve's way was to swallow a new idea and digest it. His reaction to Colt's reason for moving down to the second floor dorm was delayed for weeks. Then late one night, when Steve had noticed the trouble Colt was having with the multiple assignments of the enthusiastic faculty, Steve asked, "You still going out for that election business that Master Harty wished on you?"

Colt nodded. "I owe it to him."

Steve was not convinced. "It's a holdup, man. Plain robbery. Doesn't Harty know you can't rope two horses at once?"

"I owe him a try."

Steve shook his head. "I'm disappointed in Harty. He oughtn't to ask it. No man can eat dinner for another."

"You have to pay your way," Colt said.

"You have to keep *headin'* your way, or you lose the trail. Didn't you ever notice that when you take one step in a direction, the next is easier?"

"I talked it over with Mr. MacQuarrie. He said try it. He said he'd found that when you helped somone it usually turned out you were helping yourself."

"All right, I'm a mule. When you turn off your trail because someone asks it, it only lays you open for the next request. I've worked with Easterners."

That was Steve's way of saying "period: end of trail." And presently something happened which seemed to back

Steve up in his hard-won, practical wisdom. Master Harty called Colt into his office at recess at the first opportunity after vacation and said, "With your permission, I'm asking Brick Evans to nominate you for Council in the coming election, Colt."

This jolted Colt to the bone. "I thought I agreed only to run for Student Body President," he said abruptly.

"I should have mentioned that you'd have to make Council as a preliminary. You could hardly qualify in the S.B.P. race without a working knowledge as a council member. The opposition would make hay of that lack."

Colt was jarred into silence. What a laugh Steve would have at his being taken! Harty was watching him. "I know you balk at giving this time, my friend. But education is largely knowing people. It helps you to get along with all kinds of people. It's a prime essential. The lone wolf era is gone forever."

"What about the loving?"

"There ain't no sech animal. You mean Steve, of course."

"I had Steve in mind. He's your lone wolf modern style. He likes people, he loves life, he doesn't wish harm to anyone, but he's still shy of traps. They're the things set to catch you if you step aside from your own mapped-out course. This school calls them extracurricular activities. I think Steve's got something."

Harty nodded. "Steve's also got the uneducated man's habit of condemning action wholesale, without qualification. He's right, if he's talking about the boy who rushes into so many extracurricular activities that he neglects his work.

54

What he hasn't tumbled to yet is the fact that an action is good for you if it makes you bigger than you were."

"I think Steve does that to me by just being himself."

"One extreme is as bad as another, Colt," Harty said with vigor. "You can't bargain with selfishness and get the best of the bargain. I've kept a finger on your pulse. You're doing all right. Now let me put Brick up to nominating you and you'll find you're richer by a whole new perspective of your fellows. Believe me, it's valuable. And we'll both keep an eye on your work."

"All right, I'll try."

"Good, and just one more request. Go out for baseball."

Colt flamed as if Harty had thrown a match into oil. "Good grief!" he exclaimed angrily. "What next? My shirt?"

"You came here to learn," Harty said quietly. "I'm offering you some special tuition free of cost because I think you can use it. Do you want to be a real man?"

Colt stood at the crossroads of another decision. Harty waited confidently; he knew what he was banking on. Their eyes met, and Colt's held their own against the searching ones that did not waver, either. "You win—again," he said.

Harty held out his hand. "We—it's we. Of course you mayn't be elected."

*   *   *   *   *

Savey joined Colt on the cinder path to the Gym and walked beside him as an equal. His inner change rivaled tadpole into frog, unhatched egg to chick. By the magic of being accepted in the inner circle ruled by Vance, Savey's shell was broken, and thanks to his usefulness as Dalton's tutor, his confined nature was released.

The new birth did more than straighten Savey's spine. Successive flashes showed him how much bigger school life was than he had supposed. Before he had felt at home with the wise boys, Ironwood had been a place of books, exams, and college entrance requirements. It had been only a set of decorous activities and rules, where most of the boys regarded lessons as a chore and the girls were a race apart.

Now, thanks to the underground with its terminus in Room 21, school was conspiracy, rule-busting, wild laughter and wild talk, sports, close-ups of girls that were sacrilegious but educational, close-ups of the faculty that were exaggerated but funny.

Things went on that Savey had never dreamt of and were certainly not written on the boys' faces. Vance, Hobey, Bellman, Tracy, and even Adamly, had admirable faces, quite contrary to the rules. They should have resembled malefactors, and perhaps Bill Ordley and Nick Dorritt did show signs of a lower nature. But it was remarkable how warmly likeable these delinquents could be, when they so desired, or were ordered to by Vance. Savey never suspected the briefing that Vance had given his squad of subversives about the brainy new recruit, and was intensely happy.

Henry Vanner's sharpening eye noted the new alignment with misgivings. The dean of boys had all along contested Harty's conviction that Savey could room with Satan without becoming contaminated.

Harty tried to reassure him saying, "Savey's been too deeply grounded in what's right to be uprooted by a little gaiety. Exposure to Vance and his crowd will broaden him.

After all, part of growing up is to learn to gauge human beings rightly."

"I don't believe in touching pitch to see if it does defile."

"Were you free of all misbehavior in school, Henry?"

"No, but I don't think the jumping over the traces did me any good. Do you advocate that your boys lie a little, steal a little, and bully the innocent a little to learn life?"

"You know I don't, so why try to drive me into that corner?" Harty looked at his over-serious dean with new doubt. "We're trying to teach them to see beneath the rules to the reasons for the rules. We exhort them *not* to lie, because it's unjust and cowardly; *not* to steal, because it's wrong and injures thief and victim alike; *not* to bully, because it, too, is cowardly and unjust. But we're certainly not going to fence the innocents off from the crowd and experience. If Savey gets exhilarated by his over-joyous companions to the point of inhaling or imbibing, I shan't wring my hands."

"You wouldn't dare say this in Assembly," Vanner protested.

"Simply because some of the boys have not reached your age of perception," Harty retorted warmly. "Moving Savey in with Vance was well-weighed, and a risk. A conviction that isn't a risk is hardly worth noticing. And please notice the results already. Savey has become aware of Colt Muir and Steve Livey and Brick Evans. He's got self-confidence. If a boy doesn't try out his goodness against real life, it goes flabby. Savey'll get mauled, but I'm betting he won't be knocked out. And then I count on him taking a firmer stand than he could before."

Vanner walked away unconvinced, but if Savey could

have overheard Harty's remarks about him, he would have agreed. He had no intention of disgracing his family, though he realized the danger. Already he was winking at rule-breaking by others, and it required rather unconvincing arguments with himself to adjust his conscience to its blindfold role of bystander. But what could he do? Nothing, except keep in touch with his old self and do nothing to make it reproach him. Instinctively he sought a stronger one than himself to hold to, if a showdown came. It was then he had become aware of Colt, the self-contained, strong Scot.

Savey had heard Colt maligned by Vance and Hobey, and again instinct told him to discount their views. Savey was unaware as yet that you could see a person precisely as you wished, and he was puzzled by Vance's obtuseness. Why was Vance so bitterly against Colt being elected to Council? It seemed to Savey that Colt was just the man for that job—he thought of Colt as a young man rather than a boy. Colt was steady, slow to anger, just, and a supporter of Ironwood. Savey's inward monitor told him to know Colt better.

So now, as his feet fell in step with Colt's on the cinder path Savey hinted that he would vote for Colt and gave reasons. Colt was surprised at approval from anyone even partially under Vance's thumb, but edged away from the personal by saying, "I'm learning that school's more than just cracking a book, Savey."

"I'm learning that too," Savey confided.

"So I observe." Colt turned his blue eyes on Savey's smooth, innocent face with hidden humor. "Just at present, it's trying to please that grizzly bear, Coach Kress."

"I'm still pretty scared of him," Savey confessed.

"He's a fair bear, anyway. But he mistakes basketball for my lifework."

"Bellman says you're a natural," Savey was glad to repeat.

"I'd hate to disappoint Bellman," Colt said drily.

The several teams in the long lockerroom were changing into basketball uniforms. The angry buzz of the groups told Savey that the news had reached them. Sid Dalton had failed his English test hopelessly, and was on the List.

The List! It was the Ironwood equivalent of the medieval dungeon. It meant no participation in sports with other schools. It meant afternoon study under supervision. For Sid, the backbone of the varsity squad, it was a kind of death. With Cecil Maxton as jailer, it looked like death for keeps. Sid had tried his best, had been tutored by the finest, and the English classics might as well have been written in Russian.

As Savey reached his locker, Coach Kress came out of his office, walked past the half-dressed players gathered about Vance, and said, "More speed and less talk," and walked on.

"He's in an ice-cold rage," Bud Tracy observed.

"There goes the game with George School," Hobey griped.

"We've got to do something," Bellman offered.

"You suggest it," Vance spat out.

"How's for showing Funny a thing or to?" Bill Ordley asked.

"Don't get cynical," Tracy put in without much knowledge of the word. "Master Ike would have other ideas."

"Master Ike's a long way off."

"Nobody's going to strong-arm Funny," Vance announced. "It'd only get us a trip home. Do you think Harty'd simply look on?"

"Funny's not that sort, anyway," Bellman added.

"Better breeze upstairs. Coach is chewing his lip," a passing senior said.

Coach Kress was indeed hot enough to smoke, if made of other material. He paced before the boys, knit his eyebrows, blew the whistle angrily to collect some players making tries at the far basket. When all had assembled he said, "You've heard the bad news. Sid will be on the List for a long time. So we will do without him."

Suddenly the compact and sinewy man lowered his voice. "You know that basketball's a lot more than shooting baskets, guarding, and passing the ball. Winning ball is the result of a frame of mind. It's not only determination, either. It's being humble enough to take instruction. It's practice of all the details that add up to skill. It's continuous honest self-appraisal instead of complacency. Now let's do something to make Sid feel good. Let's use the next three weeks for steady effort— and we *can* beat George School. Let's go."

Savey marveled at the old man's ability to make the sun come out.

*   *   *   *   *

Vance chose a different hiding-place every Friday for the illegal articles that Nicky Dorritt smuggled over from the Greek's. He was trying to find a foolproof, that is a faculty-proof spot, where a knapsack could be left without discovery.

Nicky might have been made to order for the job. He was small, quick of body and mind. He looked like an angel minus wings, though when Vance mentioned this asset to Hobey, his ex-roommate asked where he had got that close to one.

Nicky's cheeks were his embarrassment, red as an English choir boy's. It was chiefly Nicky's resentment at his looks that induced him to indulge in conduct that he heard aged one. But it didn't work. He still remained the cherub-faced innocent, and even Teacher Minnie loved him.

"Where tonight?" Nicky asked before supper. "It's going to be colder than you know what."

"Let's be bold," Vance said. "Bring the shoes to my room," They always called the smuggled stuff shoes.

"I suppose you know that Mr. Smith's sore as a snappin' turtle," Nicky went on. "He says you got to order more, or else."

"Tell Mr. Smith to keep his maggoty Greek temper under control. We're doing all right for a start."

"I never made eight bucks easier."

"Keep watching," Vance cautioned and handed Nicky the list. It was in code, with harmless words, such as *chewing gum, tooth paste* and *pocket comb* standing for articles that would have turned Master Ike's hair. If by any chance a boy actually wanted chewing gum, the word was underlined. Otherwise it meant Chesterfields.

Vance set off to find Hobey to remind him that they were attending faculty meeting that evening—at one remove.

6 -

Savey as Serpent

For once Vance and Hobey reached their hearing-aid before the faculty meeting was called to order. The tunnel was stifling.

"Next year we'll have to air-condition this place," Vance said.

"Next year we'll know enough to be on the faculty," Hobey amended. "Does Savey ask what you're doing out so much?"

"He knows better than to ask. I had to pinch him off quick a couple of times. Now he's stopped nosing around."

"Savey's too smart for our own good," Hobey warned. "He'll smell rats sooner or later. Either this or our tie-in with Alcibiades, or the smoking room."

"Savey knows I use the weed," Vance replied. "He hasn't ratted on that. I've got him sliding downhill, not too fast, and he likes it. He sits in at a bull session once in a while."

"But doesn't open his jaw."

Vance laughed. "Well, it'll take him a while to catch up. Sshh! Here's Harty."

The jabber of many tongues dwindled into quiet. "Hope you brought a midnight snack." Harty's jovial tones smote the boys' eardrums. "We've enough on the agenda to last till daybreak. So I ask you to remember that brevity is the short cut to bed. Lola Wilson has a worry. Is the library a spot for daters or a workshop for the advancement of tomorrow's lessons?"

A laugh tittered around the room. "They've heard this before," Hobey translated.

"If we assign them *Romeo and Juliet,* should we censure the kids for a little laboratory work?" came over the wire.

"What do you know!" Vance exclaimed. "Teacher Genevieve is making a joke."

"It's only logical, certainly," sounded the scholarly voice of Irving Cliff who headed the English department.

"They're learning how to concentrate," Coach Kress put in. Hobey and Vance hugged themselves, and Vance said, "They're taking a poke at Little Iceberg, that's all. They don't mean it."

They heard Cecil Maxton's crisp speech. "*We're* not being logical, at any rate. We tried the first day to get the boys and girls together, now we do nothing but try to keep them apart."

The Green Room hee-hawed at that, and then Harty doubled the laughter by saying, "Must we restrict Savey Miller's liberty?"

"They sure are out to get Little Iceberg's goat," Hobey said.

"All right, all right," came Lola's clear voice. "I was wrong to bring it up."

"No, you were not!" came the ominous staccato of Teacher Minnie Winters. "In my thirty years of attendance at these meetings, I've never heard so disgraceful a levity."

"I'll say!" commented Hobey. "Boy, this is worth smothering for."

Minnie went on, "It is a fortunate thing that the children cannot hear your childishness."

"Now we're set," Vance chuckled. "All right, Min, talk me to sleep."

"Lola is profoundly right. The school should provide separate hours for boys and girls in the library. We will forfeit all claims to discipline if this behavior is allowed to go on behind the Encyclopedia Britannica. When I came to this Quaker institution, the very word 'dating' had not been heard. It has made the word 'lady' obsolete. The customs of vulgarity encroach day by day. I wish you could hear what passes for conversation in what they call, with superlative vulgarity, bull sessions."

"Should be 'cow seances,' " Hobey suggested.

Master Harty interposed. "We, too, have an interesting vocabulary at our end of the building, but let us restrict our attention to the library. We cannot have separate hours. It is well to recall Master Isaac's basic dictum: self-discipline is our goal. I prefer a little kicking over the traces to rules so strict they weaken the individual's will. Let the Honor List tell. As I mail it each month to Master Isaac, I compare it with last year's List, and we're doing quite as well. The situation is all my fault, anyway. As dean of admissions I've enrolled girls who are far too beautiful and vivacious. They make me feel as if I just didn't want to be forty-two."

A wave of laughter broke on the microphone in the Green Room organ and Vance said, "Good old Harty. He never will admit that it's wrong to live."

"I can hardly wait until Master Isaac returns from this ill-advised leave," Teacher Minnie said and sat down.

"If there's no further light on the library dilemma," Harty said, "we'll pass to an even more sinister problem. Let me try to state it fairly. Sid Dalton is on the List because Master Cecil's efforts to open his mind to the fundamentals of English needed to pass the College Boards have been in vain. Coach Kress believes that we should examine this case."

"Do you know, I think they ought to broadcast these faculty meetings," Vance said. "They're the real stuff."

They heard Kress expel the air through his nostrils like a bull moose and say, "I wish to state that I know Master Cecil is within his rights. From his point of view, Sid should be on the List. But Master Cecil is a newcomer, and I've been seeing this situation arise for thirty-five years. I've seen Master Ike deeply troubled by his inability to know where justice lies.

"Sid Dalton is a good boy. He works hard for me and for his teachers, including Master Cecil. He gets B's and C's in most subjects, but is weak in languages. I don't think they'll keep him out of a good college, and I'm sure they won't keep him out of his father's lumber business. He talks and writes well enough to be understood. Why not realize that he won't master the fine points of Milton and Shakespeare. Why must he? Why should we be all alike?"

"Cecil, your answer," Harty said.

"I ask other questions," came the young, confident voice. "Am I hired to give up Sid's chance to develop his mind in an important phase of education? Am I hired to compromise on a question of favoritism and wink at the failure of our most conspicuous athlete? Shall I meekly grant privileges to our star that are denied to boys with inferior muscle? Obviously I intend to answer *No*. Sid is capable of meeting my requirements if he will set aside his dislike of concentrating on them. Since the List is my only weapon, I propose to wield it until Headmaster Isaac Ironwood orders otherwise."

The boys heard a solitary clapping and Teacher Minnie's voice, "Thank goodness someone on the staff has a stout spine."

Coach Kress interrupted. "I object at the innuendoes just expressed. First, as to favoritism. Boys know justice. They are sensitive to injustice, especially when it works against them. Yet I've never heard one boy complain in a case like this. As for winking, I protest at this accusation. At worst, we are making a tacit exception. It is a working compromise, well understood by the student body, in so clear an instance as Sid, yet remains tacit because circumstances vary. I would be willing to submit our case to Council, which is composed with one notorious exception, of hard-thinking boys who maintain a remarkable level of honesty."

"I decline this new compromise," Cecil said. "Boys naturally do not complain when a key athlete, like Sid, is allowed to play, though against our specified rules. The reason is that boys are largely opportunists. A baby is 100% opportunist. Some boys mature earlier and view decisions from a wider point of view. But in the main, they have not yet devel-

66

oped standards. Now either one has standards or one hasn't them. I have imagined that Ironwood School's chief job was to develop standards. Therefore I am unwilling to hand over my responsibility to a group of schoolboys. This is one matter in which my opinion is fixed."

"I approve!" Teacher Minnie cried happily.

"And I," "And I" came from other feminine voices.

"And I," Henry Vanner echoed. "I was not here last year but it seems to me that if the List-cure had been strongly applied to Sid then, and the year before, this question would not arise now. He is still a junior. Let us be firm now. Then next year he may be able to blossom out as super-athlete again on an honest basis."

"I hear a lot over the transom, Cecil," Kress said. "The boys accuse you of riding Sid unmercifully. Why, for instance, do you lay such a particular emphasis on irony? I'm not very clear on that myself."

"Because irony is so prominent in our modern life."

"For example?"

"As when a member of the staff argues against teaching."

Vance roared. "Coach took that one on the chin," he said. "You know, Hobe, Funny's got a razor-edge mind, and I don't mean a safety."

"You don't need to tell him," Hobey said. "Anything for a laugh at somebody else's expense. He got the women with him that time."

"Let me put the question," Harty was saying. "Shall we back Cecil in his scrupulous literalness of the rule that marks below 60 automatically forfeit athletic participation with outside schools? Or shall we make a free translation of that rule in favor of a boy who admittedly works hard?"

"Exceptions tangle us in contradictions and unfairness to others," Henry Vanner said. "I am loath to grant Dalton special favors."

"I hope that we see that to be strict now with Sidney is best for him and the school in the long run," Teacher Minnie said.

Others agreed. "Is that the general sentiment of the meeting?" Harty asked. "Those in favor of the literal interpretation say aye."

The "ayes" clearly had it, and Hobey clenched his fist. "The idiots!"

"That's that," Vance said angrily. "I'll give Savey the green light."

*   *   *   *   *

Virginia Dorset Erdwin had as many reputations as a cat has lives. Outsiders were meant to envy her clothes. Girls invited to her room marveled at the pennants from colleges and the snaps of Ginny with handsome boys in summer garb. Diane Ebbitts, her roommate, was granted a special peek at a photograph of Sid and Ginny in an affectionate attitude under a grape trellis.

Diane knew a thing or two herself. She showed this picture to Sid, much to his embarrassment. He was too polite to tell Diane that it was a composite, a fake, but Diane gathered as much and wisely did not mention the incident. As for the pennants, she knew that the enterprising Woolworth concern sold them for a dollar.

The boys knew a good deal about Ginny, too. This was

not surprising since she devoted her many talents to that end —at least before Vance took over. He undoubtedly knew Ginny better than anyone else, for he had reconnoitered for months before closing in. He valued highly her sense of humor and her revolutionary urge, so like his own, though more cunning and less principled. He was irked by her independence when he wanted her to agree. But Vance knew the value of a dissenting opinion. Above all, Ginny was that rarity, a detective in skirts; also, she could keep a secret as long as she wished.

They had several meeting-places for the exchange of campaign strategies: at dances; at the school store during recess; in that lovers' shrine, the Library, where Teacher Lola seasoned the fun with warnings; and—for important arguments—that sheltering nook under the library stairs.

Vance summoned Ginny to the stairs the day after the faculty meeting about Sid. There he explained the system of Savey's plan which was to go into effect on Monday.

"Did Savey actually dream that up?" Ginny exclaimed under her breath. "Why, bless his little head! But Savey, of all boys! I thought he wouldn't do anything Teacher Minnie wouldn't."

"Savey's coming along," Vance granted.

Ginny laughed soundlessly. "Vance, you're a genius. I'm afraid of you."

Vance warmed at this praise. It confirmed his judgment. Anybody could fall for the girl's profusion of date-blonde hair, her flawless complexion, so innocently roselike, and her mind, which was neither. But it had taken his insight to realize her true gifts, for conspiracy and carrying on his good works. "I didn't have anything to do with this," he said generously. "Savey's got that kind of a brain. It takes things apart. He thinks we can do it in a month. Either Funny will see the light, or out he goes."

"He's the original serpent, Savey is."

Vance noticed the dean of boys through the bannister and said, "I've an errand at the store and need your advice. Meet me there in five minutes."

Ginny was punctual and found Vance staring at shelves laden with food that girls devoured between meals. "I want to give your helpers a feed," he said. "Pick out what you think the girls would like. I'll try not to look."

"Oh, Vance, you don't have to do this. Diane and Edna and Lorna will be crazy to try it. They all love Sid, though I think Edna has a crush on Master Cecil—that little mustache."

"I'd like to shave it off," Vance said. "Now pick out a good feed."

"Your parents suddenly double your allowance?"

"Nope, I've been saving up—for emergencies like this."

Ginny remembered something and her smile faded. "Where were you the night before vacation ended, Vance?"

Vance's practice in not revealing his emotions paid off at Ginny's thunderbolt. Why this interest in ancient history? His mind instantly repeated its favorite question: *what did she know?* "I was visiting Hobe? Why?"

"Diane called Hobey's house and they said he was visiting you. So she phoned your house and they said you were visiting Hobey. She had sense enough not to tell what she'd heard. How about coming clean?"

Ordinarily Vance would have kept the girl guessing, as a

matter of principle. It paid off in so many ways. But now he must quash this nosey probe at once and lowered his voice. "Hobe and I were seeing the town, Gin. Kindly keep it under the hair-do."

"Which town?" Ginny's reason for wanting to know went deeper than Vance imagined. She was more serious about this dark boy of courage and imagination and humor and good looks than she liked to admit.

"New York," Vance whispered. "Now will you stow it?"

"Oh," Ginny breathed unhappily. She applauded Vance's vendetta against rule and the faculty's narrow-mindedness, yet she could not bear to find him really loose, really bad. With Hobey, badness would be weakness. But not with Vance. He did not yield to temptations, he planned them.

Ginny felt like putting the chocolates and stuff back on the shelves. Why did Vance keep their evening dark, if there was nothing to hide? She could not endure having Vance set up this high fence between them. She wanted to cry out, "You ask me to do a job for you, and when I ask you—because I want to know everything about you, for a special reason, you slam the door. It's not fair."

But Ginny hadn't yielded to such childishness as that since she was fourteen, and now she contented herself with saying, "I'll talk to the girls tonight and let you know. And thanks, Vance, so much for the marshmallows and pop."

*   *   *   *   *

Ginny waited until the three girls had been sufficiently sweetened by Vance's offerings before springing Savey's scheme. The girls were comfortable in pajamas, it was late enough to be interesting, and Ginny's news was exciting.

"It won't work," said Edna Hallett, who mixed some brains with her social ambitions. "Funny's just not that dumb. Andy Bellman gets nothing but A's. How's he going to pull himself down to D's without Funny smelling a rat?"

"Savey's master-minding this," Ginny said. "We're to make our mistakes so gradually, and over a whole month, so that Funny will be frustrated. Bellman won't be poor every day. Savey may allow him to be brilliant once a week, but on that day two of us will say 'unprepared' and draw a goose egg. See?"

"There are such things as reports," Diane asked. "Has Savey a way of staving off parents?"

"It's only for a month, one report," Ginny said patiently. "You will be furnished with excuses. Savey's thought of everything. And there is such a thing as patriotism, Di. We're doing this so that Sid can get back into the game before we play Westtown. Who was the hero in Roman History IV who jumped into the chasm to save something or other?"

"Forget the chasm," Lorna cut in. "It's a beautiful idea and I love Savey for thinking of it."

"Is Colt going along?" Edna asked.

"Colt's not to know. Nobody's to know," Ginny said with emphasis. "But especially not Colt."

"How can he help knowing?" Edna persisted. "I don't mind going along for Sid, but I don't want to go blind."

"Don't worry, nobody's ever accused you of that," Diane said and the others laughed.

"Our mistakes are going to be so *natural,*" Ginny said, "that neither Colt nor Funny can guess. It's like a play, see?"

72

"I just love being an actress," Lorna said. "It's terrible to think of Sid sitting on the sidelines all winter."

"I just *hate that man!*" Diane broke out. "And that baggy sweater."

Ginny hoped that Edna would let this pass for Sid's sake and said, "Vance says he's going to book a passage for Funny back to England for March 15th."

The girls screamed with delight. Then Ginny said in parting, "Not one word, one look, or one smile. And remember never, *never* to be amused at Funny's cracks, especially against Sid."

"Who wants to?" Lorna asked.

"Won't it give us away, if we never smile?" Edna asked.

"Savey says Funny'll only think us dumb and that makes our mistakes more natural," Ginny said. "Savey's giving the most of all, for he's never failed to make the Honor List. We've got to be *nice* to him for this."

"Corney will see to that" Diane said.

7 -

Vance Needs a Loan

For half a century George School, Westtown School, and Ironwood had battled for the acknowledged supremacy in sports that winning teams give. The three Quaker strongholds were so evenly supplied with athletes that no winning streak lasted for long. Now, as Coach Kress watched his tense five play its first game against George School's unbeaten team, he bit his lips and vowed a vow that had been pushed aside by Captain Sid Dalton's dazzling activities on the soccer field, the basketball floor, and the baseball diamond.

"Never again, never again," the strong man muttered. "I'll be blamed if I will." The vow pertained to the temptation offered by star players. It was so easy to relax and let them do it. And then they broke a leg, or got a virus, or sat there on the sidelines like Sid because they thought William McKinley was prime minister of England.

Kress had tried not to glance at Dalton. It made him furious to see Captain Sid watching his team fly to pieces in the first period that was just ending. Kress had brought Andy

Bellman's six foot of muscle and scholarship to take Sid's place at left forward. But Bellman was sensitive, high-strung, and communicated his jitters to every play.

Vance, the other forward, was taut. He had imagination, too. He missed his tries with singular precision. Hobey relapsed into sightlessness at right guard, and when he did remember to pass the ball it was to some waiting George School player. Bud Tracy was nearly as upset at left guard. Bill Ordley had started at center, but felt sick to his stomach, and was replaced by Brick Evans.

Kress bit his lips steadily as the first period failed to end the natural tension that the big games invariably set up. The score stood: George School 21, Ironwood 8—a proof of demoralization that bewildered the three hundred spectators. It was a shot in the arm for the visitors, who had boasted that they had come to clean up after two years of Ironwood victories, but really doubted it. Demoralization persisted, and the half ended 31 to 15.

Dalton rose to go downstairs with the team, but Kress saw Martha Cording sitting as near as a girl could get to the players. Martha was not only a delight to look at, but a miracle of self-effacement rare in any young woman of seventeen. She was as openly happy about Sid as Sid was about sports. She seemed content to play second fiddle to a baseball mitt. Her dating was a masterpiece of good taste and her seemingly chief desire was to be sure that Sid got enough sleep. Harty had once summed up the affair to Kress in a phrase. "They've been dating since ninth grade and will continue until their golden wedding anniversary."

Kress said to Sid, "Martha wants to speak to you, Sid,

and I want to put the boys to sleep. So stay up here. The game isn't lost yet."

"Tell Vance . . ." Sid stopped and then said, "Make Vance captain in my place, Coach. That'll steady him."

"I know what I'm going to tell Vance—to shut his eyes when he tries for the basket. The ball knows." With this witticism between experts, Kress beckoned Martha to advance and went below.

Colt had gone down with the boys although he had little chance of playing, and the dressing room struck him as a morgue. The winded remains strewn on the rubbing tables made him feel out of place.

Kress acted busy. He knew better than to scold; this was too serious. He let five minutes pass without a word.

"Gosh, why doesn't he start in on us?" Hobey whispered to Vance.

"He's the devil, that's why," said Tracy who was almost in tears. "He wants to grind it in."

"I told Ordley to lay off the weed," Vance said. "He's been hitting a pack a day."

"Don't mention that mongrel or I'll be sick, too," Bellman said. "May all dogs pardon me for the comparison."

Somebody snickered, and Vance said, "Hobe's the one to be sorry for. His present date, three of the past and two of the future, were all looking at him. He'll probably leave the school."

"Only if you stay," Hobey said bitterly, and then the ultimate insult occurred to him. "George School ought to give you a scholarship after what you've done for them."

"Sshh!" Bellman cautioned as Kress neared. Five min-

76

utes of limp relaxation can do wonders to the well-trained, and Kress judged the soil ready for sowing. "Forget it," he said brusquely. "You've just as much time ahead as you've had. Stop playing for yourselves. Play for the basket and for each other. Tracy, watch the ball all the way into your hands. Vance, talk it up. Bellman, stop charging. Hobey, keep your temper. Your man's out to get it. Brick, you're doing all right, but let yourself go more.

"Now for the other team. They'll be walking on air. They'll be overcareful. This is your period. Dedicate it to Sid. He's out there, and you know how he feels. Make it up to him. Now play as if each minute was the last you have to score."

Colt could see the team visibly pull itself together. The five walked up the stairs in a new mood. Colt marveled at the man who could stay the tide of their nervousness single-handed. He went back to his seat beside Steve Livey, who was not in uniform because of a strained ankle, and said, "Kress did it."

"I believe you," Steve said drily. "But thousands wouldn't." The whistle blew and he added, "They're off like a herd of turtles."

But he was wrong. It might be slow motion, it was calculated motion, and Ironwood began to score quick tries in succession. It required only two or three to ignite the watchers. Vance sank two foul shots and made two baskets, and the Ironwoodies rose, roared, shouted and screamed. The score was 31 to 25 before George School took the lead again.

Then Hobey retrieved all errors by a scoring streak of his own, bringing the total to 33 for George School, 30 for

77

Ironwood. The Ironwood passes flew true, the Ironwood ball did what was expected of it and stopped rimming the basket as before. A brilliant throw by Bellman tied the score. Colt caught sight of Neil MacQuarrie's tense but shining face, then salvos of shouts brought him back to the game. Tracy had made it 34 for Ironwood to 33 for the rivals. Bedlam, happiness, immortal hope!

The whistle declared the period over. "That goes down in history," Steve said to Colt.

Then the reaction. The George School team, shattered with surprise, got its feet under it again in the final period, while Ironwood tried too hard. Tracy fell and gashed the skin above an eyebrow so deeply that the blood interfered with his game. Morley replaced him only to sprain an ankle. Stenson replaced Morley and the mood was broken. Vance sprawled headlong, rose and slugged the George School forward who, in Vance's opinion, had charged him. It was the crisis of the struggle. The foul gave the visitors two free throws, the loss of Ironwood's most skillful player, and the game. Ironwood 39, George School 51.

Kress was never abler than in defeat. He moved about the lockerroom, which was singularly quiet, except for the hiss of the half-dozen showers and occasional monosyllabic retorts. He asked about near-injuries, commented on the inspired playing of the third quarter, and ended with, "We can still get back at them by beating Westtown. If you fellows can be just half as good in every quarter as you were in the third quarter today, we can lick any high school team in the East."

Colt hurried into his clothes and caught up with Ellen

Waring. It was a comfort to have her sympathy to turn to. Her first remark was typical of Ellen's mature reaction to the life about them. She wasted no time on the school's disappointment but went at once to the personal hurt that needed soothing. "Poor Vance!" she said. "I know how he feels."

"It was inexcusable, Ellen," Colt said. "He knew he was king pin, with Sid out. But he refused the responsibility."

"Yes, but he's proud, for all that."

"It's the rest of us I feel sorry for," Colt said. "We just might have copped the game. Then Vance threw the chance away."

"I know, but there are three hundred of us, Colt, while Vance must know all you say and suffer horribly alone."

Colt met the eyes turned upward with a slight smile. "There aren't enough underdogs to keep you happy, Nell," he said and wanted to add, "I love you for it," but forbore. They were surrounded at the exit by listeners.

"Just the same, I hope you aren't going to furnish me with another," Ellen said with a fine light in her eyes. "I mean about the Council election."

"I'm in," Colt said quietly. "The voting was after lunch."

"And you didn't tell me!"

He grinned. "I was coming to it. It was closer than the game. I had one vote lead."

"How splendid!" her low tones thrilled him. She made it seem a victory for both of them.

"How surprising!" His grin widened.

"Not to me."

"Now teach me the alphabet, Nell. My mind's full of

79

large open spaces about the job. It can't be anything anybody wants, or they wouldn't have shoved it at me."

They had emerged into the pale February sunshine, but the light managed to hint of something beyond winter. They turned aside from the others, and Ellen said, "It *is* responsibility, of course, and only a few are willing to accept that side of it, though many would like the honor. People aren't used to being alone with themselves any more, Colt. I think that's the first thing Council does to you. You learn what it is to be alone, with only yourself to advise and help. But that will be nothing new to you."

He was grateful to her for her understanding of the little he had told her about himself, and he suddenly realized how firm was the footing of his warm regard for her.

"It was all new to me," Ellen went on. "I've been wrapped up in family and relatives and friends. I'd never imagined having to be stern with a friend or perhaps turn her in."

"I couldn't imagine you doing it."

"But you can't run with the hare and hunt with the hounds, Colt," Ellen said quietly. "Your duty as Council member comes first. If your friend has broken a rule, you have to reason with him or let him take the consequences. That's your obligation to the boys who voted you in. They've made you their conscience and their judge, and judges must have integrity."

Colt whistled. "Well, maybe there's enough Scot in me to do it."

"The hardest thing for me is to be loyal to a Council decision."

"But suppose they vote the earth flat again? Must I agree?"

Ellen laughed. "That's where the faculty advisor comes in. You're lucky in having Master Blaik. He will convince them that the earth's shape isn't subject to their vote, perhaps, or get them back on the rails some other way. You'll find working with Master Blaik one of the unadvertised rewards of being on Council. Master Ike sees to it that the very finest man and woman he has are elected to advise these pets of his, the two Councils. And there's another unadvertised reward. By sticking up for what's right you never lose the respect of anyone who counts."

"That's Mr. MacQuarrie's big word, *respect*. Now what else?"

Ellen laughed again. "It's no pill you're opening your mouth for, Colt. It's insight into people. A place on Council is a ringside seat on human nature. You'll be surprised at what comes up. I'm only sorry you won't see Council as it should be."

Colt knew that she was referring to Ordley but said nothing. They had reached the Hall and he squeezed her hand good-by. Ellen responded and said, "I'm so glad, Colt, and you will be too. In a month. You'll see. Will you tell me?"

He nodded and was glad, too. It meant that he and Ellen had something important in common.

*　　*　　*　　*　　*

Savey lay on the upper bunk of the two-tiered beds in a helpless rage. He would drowse off and then be jolted awake by a sharp laugh or a suppressed snarl from the endless game.

It must be 2 A.M. and the four of them, Vance, Hobey, Ordley and Tracy, had been at it since lights out. Savey wished he had the guts to order them out of his room and sound convincing. They would only laugh at him and deal again.

In a fury unnatural to him, Savey almost hoped that Master Henry would catch them and give them the book. But he took that back. He owed Vance too much. His hand felt under his pillow for the precious notebook. He was forever in debt to Vance and the others for the riches compiled between the limp black covers of that treasury of secret knowledge.

There were many kinds of bull sessions, Savey discovered. Occasionally one was loud, disputatious, and very funny.

Unfortunately these noisy meetings were always short. The Chief Proctor or his assistants usually overheard the hilarity before it penetrated to official quarters and took steps. Alas, the humor was too fast and simultaneous for Savey to take notes, and the warm-hearted laughter was the best of it, anyway.

There was the bull session most of which was serious and respectable. Half a dozen of Vance's cronies would join the shadows on the floor to discuss some burning occurrence of the day. A faculty member would be taken apart, or some Saturday evening program torn to pieces. Eventually the talk got to girls and yielded Savey pages of notes. His hearing was quick to catch the wisdom imparted in undertones, and the twilight of one candle was enough to guide his pencil.

Savey was no callow youth. He knew the conventional facts about girls and was widely read. Yet now he felt himself merely a tourist in this other country where Vance and his friends appeared so much at home. Soon Savey's practical streak, which ran like a scarlet thread through his idealism, realized that here, in these experienced boys' talk, there was a second schooling, not mentioned in the Ironwood Catalogue, and tuition free. At once a scheme to make astute use of the knowledge being thrust upon him was born in his agile mind. He bought the notebook the next day.

It was soon half-filled with jottings of success and failure, of experiment and frustration, and all of immediate interest to anyone who yet lacked access to this information. Savey had once bought for ten cents a worn copy of a textbook entitled "How to Win Friends and Influence People." He had heard of its immense sale. Why shouldn't he publish a similar textbook for boys in the same class of ignorance as his recent self? Boys unsuspecting the finer points of social behavior? Boys who yearned as he had once, before Lola Wilson had introduced Cornelia, for a real date.

The idea seemed purest inspiration from a Higher Sphere, and Savey was smart enough to know when to be secretive. His notebook was the shaft opening down to a gold mine if only he could work it. Suddenly the hardships of being kept awake resolved into Opportunity. By Easter he might be an author, and by June he might be rich. So glistening a prospect had never lighted his day dreams before. And now it was possible!

"Come down off that roost and join the gang, Save," Vance invited once in a generous mood.

Savey pleaded sleep since he could not tell the truth— that he was making too much money in taking down their wisdom.

Even on this tedious night he had covered three pages with rare expressions born of the earnest game. Then the need to sleep forbade sharp attention. He was aroused for the twentieth time by whispers, threats, promises, and then it was over. The opened door indicated stealthy exits. But he, alas, had been jarred out of any possibility of slumber by learning that Vance had lost an enormous sum of money to Bill Ordley.

"You awake, Save?" Vance asked in a hoarse whisper.

"Half," Savey murmured. "Maybe a third."

"How much money you got handy? I owe Bill fifty-five bucks."

"Fifty-five *dollars*?" Savey was staggered.

"It was only twenty-seven fifty till the last throw. How about a little loan?"

"But my whole term's allowance is only ten dollars, and that's half gone already."

"Bill says he'll ask my dad for it if I don't start paying tomorrow. Pop'd go up in the air like a bomb. Wow!"

"I can lend you four dollars, Vance. I'd do anything I could. You know that."

"You're a good guy," Vance said. "I believe you would. Gosh, what a day! I lose the Council election to Colt. I lose the game to George School. And now I lose my shirt to that fourflusher."

Savey was warmed to the boiling point by Vance's faith in him. His book was now a necessity. He could visualize himself offering fifty-five dollars to Vance out of the first profits. But that was rather far off. "Bill won't tell your father," Savey said, for that was too monstrous a crime for even Bill Ordley to commit.

"He's kind of pressed himself," Vance said. "Well, give me your four bucks in the morning. I've got fifty cents, and can dredge up a few more from the fellows I don't owe. That ought to shut his mouth for a few days. Don't lose any sleep over it."

Savey restrained himself from saying that he'd been deprived of about five hours of sleep already. He felt deeply sorry for Vance. Maybe he did deserve all this, but somehow . . . The charitable qualification never reached words, for Savey slept.

*　　*　　*　　*　　*

William Keane Ordley could have signed B.M.C.—Big Man on Campus—after his name during his junior year at Ironwood—if loudness, swagger, and amazing deeds with a baseball bat were enough to win that dubious title.

Vance discovered the undercover Ordley first, in soccer, for he was on the receiving end of big Bill's surreptitious dirty-work. Ordley would do anything to win if only he could hide it. Vance checked on his findings with Hobey and Bud. Bull session analysis declared the newcomer a gold-plated punk. He was unsure at heart because he had nothing firm to stand on: no morals, no decency, and nobody but himself to play for. Yet he had tricked out these failings with gusto and cunning, a marvelous eye at bat, and a spurious heartiness that deceived the inexperienced.

Vance and Hobey were at the height of their sophomore jocularity, and went into a midnight huddle with a few they could trust. They would play an immense joke on the school and make it pay. They'd make Ordley Student Body President, and in return escape a thousand penalties and arrests. This was wickedness on a scale so dazzling and hilarious— and so helpful—that Vance hoped it would look possible by morning light.

It did. There was time enough to go at their schemes with disarming gradualness. Part of the plot was to induce Ian MacQuarrie to run. They knew he would never stoop to the campaign practices planned. Some of the faculty were taken in by Ordley's double-talk. When someone in faculty meeting prophesied that young Ordley would go far, Master Harty concurred with, "Indeed he will—in the wrong direction. I ask the school's pardon for admitting him, son of a mayor though he is."

The impossible happened. "The flaw must lie with us," Isaac Ironwood said sadly. "When the boys can choose Ordley over Ian MacQuarrie, we have failed them somehow."

"Boys are still boys," Kress put in. "Not venerable justices of the Supreme Court. I admit Bill dazzled me at first. Take a star soccer player, a star basketball player, a double-star ball player, and add the showmanship of that disastrous pair, Vance and Hobey, and the girls they enlisted to plug for their phony, and it's no wonder the kids discounted Ordley's weaknesses. Next year I vote that the candidates' campaign expenses be listed. Ordley spent a lot of money in buying this election, with Alcibiades helping."

"There's no law against feeding hungry boys," Harty said.

On that Election Night, Vance and Hobey hugged themselves. Next year they would have a hidden hand in school management. Soft and pretty! But now, in February, Vance wished he had never seen Bill Ordley. If Vance could play on Bill's weakness of spine, so could others. Master Blaik gave Bill just enough rope, then tightened the noose of law and order. Bill's father knew his son and curbed his yen for spending by withholding money.

On the morning after Vance's bad day, Bill hunted him up and said, "I want my money today."

"Sorry, the banks are closed on Sunday."

"You can get it. Borrow it from the Greek."

Vance looked hastily around. "Shut up, you fool. Mr. Smith is his name. He's in New York, I happen to know."

"Quit stalling and start paying," Ordley said. He was taut from lack of sleep and exasperation and his eyelids felt sandy.

"I said I'd give you something on account." Vance pulled the accumulation of his efforts from a pocket. "Seven bucks."

"That's no good. I want at least half now and the rest tomorrow."

"I don't know what you're going to do about it," Vance said coolly.

"I know what you're going to do. Get it from your old man. And if you don't ask him, I will."

Vance had foreseen this talk and had his reply. "Do you want to take the same train home?"

"If you tried squealing, they wouldn't believe you."

"Oh no?" Vance smiled now. It was so obvious a trap, but Bill, for all his bluster, was such a fool. Ordley looked into the dark steady eyes and realized his emptiness.

"That's better," Vance said, seeing his victory. "Now,

I'll pay that debt. But it'll take time, and if you don't keep your mouth shut, I'll shut it for you."

"That's something you can't do," Ordley said foolishly.

"I've taken punishment before, Bill," Vance said. "For something I believed in. That's what you can't do."

"I don't know what you're talking about."

"Sure, I agree. You don't." Vance stepped closer and lowered his voice. "Get wise to yourself, if you can. Think of someone besides your lousy self, if you're able. If you get canned out of here, it'll be in all the papers. The son of the Mayor expelled! Your old man will love that! Think it over."

It was a body blow. Vance went on. "Sure, you can get me and Hobe fired, too. But our papas aren't going to run for reelection, and you're going to have two enemies for life. Think it over."

Ordley shifted back to more solid ground. "When are you going to pay?"

"I can give you four bucks a week, but only if I stay in business."

Vance left the Student Body President to get his coat. It was bad enough getting a bear by the tail. But a skunk! Then you *had* to hold on.

8 -
Sid Has a Say

"You were punk today, Bellman," Vance complained one snowy night because the recently brilliant scholar had absentmindedly replied correctly to Funny Maxton's question. "Brace up, man."

"I'm sorry," Bellman replied contritely and meant it. "It's awfully hard to be wrong so much. But I've done a rotten theme for tomorrow. The worst yet. It should rate me D minus at best."

But Tracy yelped with the idiocy of it. "I bet it's a honey."

"It's harder making good mistakes in *The Merchant of Venice* than in *Julius Caesar*," Savey said. "My homework takes twice as long."

Tracy laughed again. "Remember when I said, 'Yond Cassius has a lean and hungry mien?' Shakespeare wouldn't have been worse burnt up than Funny was."

"I had to talk you out of saying 'mug.'" Savey smiled reminiscently.

"Funny made me write 'Cassius' fifty times for spelling the guy with one 's,' " Hobey put in.

"What's your theme on?" Vance asked. He had a genuine regard for Bellman's brains and a real interest in his work, his mind. Vance felt a large gratitude to the A-plus scholar for downgrading himself for Sid's sake. It was a lot to ask of intellectual pride, and Vance took pains to show his appreciation.

"Anti-Dictatorship," Bellman said. "I start out red-hot against Hitler, Mussolini, Stalin, and their like, and gradually work in instances where I claim it's justified until I just about qualify for a seat in the Politburo."

Tracy howled, for he loved Bellman's subtle imbecility. "Imagine Andy in the Kremlin! Funny'll have a fit."

Vance was thoughtful. "I'm not sure you should hand that in, Bellman. What if Funny shows it to Harty?"

"Harty won't think Bellman's going communist," Hobey said.

"I'm not afraid of that. But what if Harty smells a rat? He knows that Bellman can't believe what he's writing and then he'll wonder whether or not Bellman's pulling Funny's leg."

"That never occurred to me," Bellman said flushing. "You're right. Gosh, all that work wasted! Why hasn't Funny tumbled to us already?"

"He's too self-satisfied to see things from another guy's point of view," Vance said.

"Colt isn't self-satisfied, yet he hasn't caught on," Bellman persisted.

"Because Colt's the best minder of his own business I

know. I've got to hand him that." Vance kept his admirers by this sort of honesty.

"Well, they must be dumb," Brick Evans said. "A quarter of the class is on the List now. Even a smart girl like Ginny."

"Savey, did you make up that definition of irony that Ginny gave last week?" Bellman asked. ". . . 'a coward's way of hinting something he's afraid to say outright.' I nearly spoiled it by laughing."

They all laughed and Savey said, "Ginny gets the credit for that."

"I thought Funny'd burst into flame," Hobey remarked.

"Something's got to break," Brick said. "The faculty won't stay fooled much longer."

"They'll decide that the man can't teach," Vance said with a grin. "They'll petition Ike to fire him by cable."

"I hope it happens before the Westtown game," Hobey said. "We've just got to have Sid back for that."

Tracy said, "I'm more worried about Sid getting on to our game than Colt. When Funny read the List, Sid said to me, 'What's the matter with you guys? Funny'll be asking me to tutor you next.' And if Sid does find out, it's curtains for all this. He'd never let us get bum marks for his sake."

"Still less have Funny fired for his sake," Brick added.

Savey was uncomfortable. "They'd never let Funny go just because one class went to pieces, would they?"

Vance looked sharply at Savey and hastily said, "No, no. We were kidding, Save. None of us wants Funny fired. Re-formed, yes."

"I'd sure like to attend the faculty meeting that thrashes it out," Tracy suggested.

Hobey and Vance were far too good actors to look at one another, but for safety's sake, Vance said, "So would I. Now get your mistakes from Save, fellows, and beat it. I've got some boning up on chemistry to do."

*   *   *   *   *

Savey could not put his conscience on ice, as Vance had suggested on another occasion. He was finding out that the way of the transgressor was tricky if not hard. He had heard his fellow conspirators talk about Funny's being fired, but had put it down to wishful thinking. Now he was worried for the first time. He must find out, for it would be awful if anybody should lose a job on his account. Savey was appalled.

Yet how could he find out without going back on his friends? And *that* was impossible. After years of being all but friendless, he could not endure cutting himself off from Bellman, who respected his brains, or from Vance who had lifted him out of his too sensitive timidity. And what would Cornelia say? He was dancing with her now, like a regular dater, sitting beside her in the dusk of the movies, holding her hand, as was required of daters and far from unpleasant.

Savey tried to shove this new anxiety out of his mind by turning to *The Merchant of Venice*. His search for possible mistakes now required an almost impossible finesse. They had to be seemingly natural mistakes that a bright boy could make. Yet the averages of Vance, Tracy, Hobey, and even Bellman were so perilously near the fatal 60 that put one on the List that Savey had to be careful not to push them over the brink. For if Vance or Hobey or even Tracy were knocked out of basketball on the approach of the Westtown game, which *must* be won, the school would demand retribution of poor innocent Funny. Irony indeed!

Savey's search for misinterpretations of Shakespeare took so much time when he wanted to go ahead with his "Guide to Girls" if that was to be his title for the work. He was working now in the Library, at a desk just behind the door where it was impossible for Teacher Lola to look over his shoulder. He had propped a tome, "*The Industrial Revolution*," in front ready to turn face down on his pages in case Lola's curiosity got the better of her manners. He dare not write in his room, lest Vance find out and laugh.

On this Friday afternoon of no games, the boys were cleaning rooms for Master Henry's inspection. Savey's orderly mind had revolutionized Vance's housekeeping. Better to pick up a dozen things today than forty tomorrow, Savey philosophized. Vance objected with, "It can't be more than so cluttered, or we couldn't get in the room." But where reason failed, example persuaded. Savey quietly picked up Vance's papers and apparel each day until Vance, less for shame than for policy, assisted. So Fridays were no longer a nightmare of digging out, but a thirty-minute job of dusting and straightening. Hobey jeered, thus confirming Vance in the new system.

Savey had the Library to himself when he heard Master Harty addressing Funny outside the door. "What news from home, Cecil?"

"Mother's no better, sir. England's having it cold."

"Bring her over here. We'll bake her. We'd be glad to have her as our guest, if she could take our savages."

"Thank you, sir. She's too infirm to travel now. More

likely I shall join her, if I find I cannot teach Americans."

Harty mentally agreed, for this vibrant, dogmatic, nice-looking scholarly graduate of Oxford, did seem unable to adapt. Why was he so reluctant to accept other customs? He still called Harty "sir" after being all but commanded not to. He still insisted on his pound of Dalton's flesh when the facts of the case had been opened to him. Now Harty said, "You'll get the hang of us Americans, sir." He lingered on that silly "sir" and watched Funny's face. It registered no change.

"On the contrary, sir, the mystery deepens," Funny said.

Harty silently agreed. Mystery hung in the air. When he passed a group in the hall, conversation paused until he was out of range. Something unmentionable was on foot. But the secret was being better kept than any in his long experience, and it was damaging the term's work.

"There's a clue somewhere," Harty said. "There always is."

"I find nothing to take hold of," Funny confessed. "One might suppose my proven ability had left me. Eleven failures in my last oral, and the averages still sagging. Yet it isn't as if they'd lost interest, rather not. They show a genuine concentration."

"Dalton's doing better, I notice."

"Only by comparison, sir, and chiefly because of the curious mistakes made by the once brighter boys, Bellman and Vance in particular. They're not silly mistakes at all, but scholarly misapprehensions of Shakespeare, made with a sort of twisted ingenuity, as if their intellects had been perverted from infancy. My predecessor must have given them the high marks which they are forever quoting at me for something else than English, their allowances or athletic ability," Funny ended bitterly.

Harty's sympathy wilted at these insulting insinuations. Funny's contention that Ironwood applied a reduced standard to athletes bit and stung. "Would it be possible that these bright boys are—well, to put it baldly, taking you for a ride, sir?" Harty intended to drive home that "sir" if it took a semester.

"A ride, sir?" Funny was puzzled. "You mean in a car?"

"I mean for a change of air and point of view, a joke."

"I've considered that, of course. I've even wondered if there might be a conspiracy to discredit me for Coach Kress's approval."

Harty shriveled some more. "But you dismissed the idea as improbable," he remarked with some sarcasm of his own.

"I was forced to by the facts. This effort is too polite for a strike. There's no hint of discourtesy. Also it is too casual. Bellman is not always stupid. Vance is even brilliant at times, as is Savey Miller."

"It is indeed inconceivable that Savey should do anything to discredit the school or you," Harty said, and Savey, behind the door, bent over his work to hide his burning face. This hurt.

"What worries me most is that similar irregularities are cropping up in my other classes. It's a sort of creeping paralysis along the English nerve. I'm losing weight. Yet their conduct remains above reproach. Before Christmas I was conscious of a trifling or a touch of rudeness. But that's past. Coupled with the failure of comprehension is a most winning air of affability. They apologize for mistakes, even offer to do extra study. I've come to the conclusion that we've never talked the same language. Certainly they haven't the perception of my classes at the old school. They are impervious to wit."

Harty's seventh sense, the schoolmaster's sense, started as if stung by a slingshot pebble. "What do you mean by wit, sir?"

Funny looked at the mirthless countenance in perplexity. Was it possible that the acting head lacked the same organ of intelligence as the boys? "Surely, sir, I need not define this commodity of the intellectual. If I make a comment in class that is—well, a shade above the pedestrian, Colt sees the wit of it and laughs, but the rest resemble your wooden Indians."

"I see," Harty said, and he supposed that he might have the mystery by the tail. "Yet Vance Draper has as keen a sense of humor as any boy I know. Nor is Hobey incapable of seeing a joke. Would you object if I drop into your class on Monday? I can sit in the rear and perhaps find a clue to the puzzle."

Savey was all ears. If Harty came, all this elaborate stupidity that he was charting for Monday was wasted. The class must behave normally. Yet that might let the cat out of the bag in one leap. No, he must organize cunning itself and fool Master Harty, too.

A new voice diverted Savey from his troubles, the husky bass of Coach Kress who had joined Funny and Harty. "I hear over the transom that you're about to put Vance and Hobey on the List, Maxton."

"That is their doing, is it not?" Funny replied icily. "I am merely the recording clerk."

"No, it's not their doing," Kress rumbled angrily. "Those boys know the Westtown game's coming up, and they'd do anything that's humanly possible to play. Wilfred, I'm glad you're here as witness. For if Maxton puts one more of my first-team boys on the List, I'm going to cable Master Ike my resignation—with reasons."

Savey heard Coach's footsteps receding and Funny's words fell into the silence: "I am equally glad that you can witness that incredible speech, sir."

"Kress has been with us quite a while, Cecil. The boys respect the very shoes he stands in."

"He means, of course, that I should cable my resignation. Well, I decline. I am fighting for a principle and the List is my appropriate weapon."

"May I be frank?" Harty asked unhappily, for he hated to say what he was now convinced he must say.

"Certainly, though I hope it is not about the holiness of athletes. I am well coached in that." His emphasis on "coached" was a knife-stab.

"Isn't the first essential to know your boy?" Harty asked with a resumed gentleness. His sympathy embraced Cecil Maxton who was so well worth a permanent place on the Ironwood staff. His forceful uprightness and his dedication to things of the intellect were needed. Yet Harty knew that he could not risk a civil war because of a refusal to consider all the facts.

"It's true that Master Ike hired you to teach English," Harty continued when Funny did not reply. "But he's equally interested in helping each boy to develop along his own unique line. Our job is to help the boy discover where his ap-

97

titude lies, and this true vocation of the schoolmaster requires a long and loving experience. Take it from me. I'm still learning. As Kress said the other day, the boys learn life partly in the classroom, partly in their sports, a good deal of it on the dorm, and no little from their dates. To shave the boys down to any one square hole maims the rounded individual we want to see emerge."

"What about Kress? He'd shave the curriculum to a point if it would help his athletes beat this blessed Westtown."

"I wish you knew George Kress," Harty said patiently. "He's simply not like that at all. He never contests the List when a boy has scanted his work. You must remember that this trouble started over Sid because you were being unduly witty at his expense. Vance has quoted some of your remarks —widely. The school is aware of your wish to be a scientist so that you could dissect Sid's brain. I believe you said it ante-dated the Neanderthal, and that he would not miss it if sold to a museum."

Funny's silence was so absolute that Savey, who was listening now without shame to the drama around the corner, held his breath. The man must say something.

"You see, Cecil?" Harty resumed almost gently. "You had Sid at a disadvantage. You cut him up and he couldn't get back at you. He hasn't Vance's wit. He probably wouldn't, anyway, for Sid Dalton's a prince. Now boys are fundamentally fair. Your sarcasm cut them up worse than it cut Sid. So if you'll reflect a little on their psychology, I think you'll begin to penetrate the mystery."

"Master Harty!" came a call along the corridor. Savey

98

recognized the voice of Miss Linbright, Harty's secretary. "Your wife's on the phone. Can you come?"

"When you're married, Cecil, you'll recognize a summons. Forgive me, if I've hurt you. I've no wish to, any more than I wish to abate your fine integrity by one jot. Nearly every problem goes deeper than is first apparent. Perhaps we should abolish the List, as you have said more than once. This stand of yours may be the finest thing for Ironwood in the year. I'll have to think it over. But do you, also, and I'll talk with Kress. Thanks.

Harty's steps faded. Savey was suspended in horror lest Funny enter the library, see him, and realize that he had heard. For an agonized minute, Funny stood still. Then he too departed.

In *The Merchant of Venice* Antonio had Portia to get him off, while who could help Savey Miller? Teacher Lola? Never. Cornelia? Hardly. Master Harty? Impossible. Vance? Worse than impossible. Then the name came. Colt. He must confide in Colt, for he was in Council. It was his duty to help the school. And Colt was different from the others—older, more experienced, and to be relied on in an awful emergency like this. Colt would listen—and wouldn't talk.

*　　*　　*　　*　　*

Savey hurried to his room to hide his efforts. He was always hiding something now. Until Vance took him in hand his life was clearest sunlight compared with the shadows of his recent existence. If being grownup meant becoming increasingly stealthy, it was a doubtful privilege.

His tutoring class was already assembled in Vance's

room. Savey had forgotten the time while eavesdropping on that terrific conversation, and he had prepared almost nothing. Also his mind was in a tremor of indecision as to what course to take next.

"You're late," Vance said.

"A little momentum, please," Bellman requested in Funny's English accents and they laughed.

The door opened again and Hobey exclaimed warningly, "Look who's here!" It was Sid, with skates hanging over his shoulder, and looking handsomer than ever because of the cold air.

"So that's what you do when you're on the List!" Tracy said enviously. "With Martha, too, I bet."

"I shall seek the List next Monday," Hobey stated.

"You will, if you don't bone up on Shakespeare," Vance said. He ignored Sid in the doorway, in the hope he'd depart.

"You've boned enough, Hobe," Sid said unexpectedly. "The game's off."

All heads twisted on their necks at this pronouncement. Bellman found his wits first and said, "You mean the Westtown game? Coach say that?"

"I mean your little game." A slow grin appeared on Sid's face. "I mean you can quit nursing me and be smart as firecrackers again."

"Come in and shut the door," Vance commanded hoarsely.

"Who told you?" Bellman demanded.

"A little bird."

"They wear skirts in winter," Hobey put in. "How did Martha know?"

Sid came in and sat on the lower bunk. "It was mighty good of you fellows," Sid said warmly. "And the girls, too."

"That was love," Tracy said with a grin. "You can discount it."

"I heard Savey started it," Sid went on, looking at the long slim boy on the floor. "I won't forget that, Save."

"Come on, cut the eulogy," Vance intruded. "Clear out, Sid. We've got to get busy. Unless you want to join in and help."

"Is it true?" Sid still looked at Savey. "Did you really teach them to make mistakes on purpose?"

"Did Funny say that?" Vance answered for Savey. "He can't teach, so he tells the girls we're making mistakes on purpose!"

"Not Funny," Sid said calmly. "A girl couldn't help hearing Ginny Erdwin coaching Lorna in her mistakes."

"That would be it!" Tracy exclaimed. "I told you what'd happen if . . ."

"Then if Funny doesn't know, we're still jake," Vance said. "Skate off to your harem, Sid, and tell them to spike the gossip."

Sid shook his head. "It's over, Vance. I won't have you or Hobe going on the List for me and ruining the team."

"Nobody's going on the List," Vance said stubbornly. "Let us manage that. Get going, will you? Gosh, we're almost there and you have to butt in. We're managing this, Sid. Now let us get on with it."

"No," Sid said with a finality that was unmistakable.

"But we've got Funny on the run. He'll be in England before he stops, if you'll kindly butt out, and you'll be playing again."

"I wouldn't want Funny fired," Sid said.

"He won't be fired," Hobey said in the effort to help.

Savey could barely breathe. If Sid won, then he need not confess to Colt, and a horrible injustice would be averted. He wondered what he could say to back up Sid. Then he remembered Harty's question. "Funny's mother's very sick," Savey contributed.

Vance shot a hot glance at this turncoat who had no nerve. "What's that got to do with it?" he demanded angrily. "All the more important for Funny to go back to her."

"You don't get it, Vance," Sid said quietly. "Your game's over, finished, done."

"I think Sid's right," came unexpectedly from Bellman. "Let's call it off. My people are yapping and it hasn't got Sid anywhere."

"Same here," Tracy added. "Dad threatens to cut my allowance until I get B's again."

"I'd rather enjoy being bright again myself," Hobe said.

The others laughed in undisguised relief at this statement. All except Vance, who said "Then we're back where we started. What becomes of Sid and the Westtown game? Look, let's give it one more week."

"No Vance," Sid said. "I thank you a lot. But not one more day."

Vance could not buck them all. "If that's the way you want it, all's jake with me."

Savey saw the fire burning back of Vance's look. When his dark eyes smoldered and his jaws firmed, watch out.

One by one the conspirators followed Sid out of the room. Even Hobey did not feel up to staying and facing the disappointed leader. When Vance was thwarted, somebody paid. Let Savey be the one. It was his fool idea, anyhow.

But Vance did not take it out on Savey when the door closed. He had other game in mind.

9 –

Trouble at the Boil

Beneath Vance's several skins lay the quivering flesh of pride. He disliked failure doubly—for its own results and because of its slap on his pride. He struck back, but not directly. On the occasion of his collapsed scheme to undermine Funny Maxton, he did not strike at Sid, or even Bellman, who had sided with Sid. His anger boiled hottest at Savey, the worm he was helping to turn into a butterfly.

When Savey had shown his disregard for Vance's wishes by that weak remark, "Funny's mother's very sick," Vance could have stabbed him. But there were subtler ways of paying this turncoat back. First it was necessary to conceal every sign of revenge, and Vance's daily contacts showed almost no change towards his roommate. Nor did he once refer to the exploded bubble, the fiasco of English V b.

In fact Savey's usefulness in that was not entirely over. It was important for the comeback to normal brilliance to be so gradual that Funny could not suspect that he had been nearly had. So, for two sessions, Savey plotted the up-curve, and gave Hobey, Tracy, Bellman, and the girls, inspired inquiries that revealed their deep interest in Shakespeare's craftmanship.

If Savey had not been so sensitive himself, he would not have felt a difference in Vance's attitude towards him. It was indefinable. Vance talked less, laughed less, and stopped wising him up about hidden motives of the faculty or women, yet so imperceptibly that Savey hardly believed his own fears. He liked Vance even more than ever for giving in about Sid so easily. He valued Vance's worldly wisdom and hoped this slight estrangement, that he imagined, was merely his imagination.

Consequently he was overjoyed, late one evening, to have the sun shine through the haze and hear Vance's old cordial voice saying, "Want to see something funny?"

Savey nodded. Any invitation from Vance was likely to open a new chapter in his life as well as being a sign of friendship.

"Ever hear of the Cellar?" Vance asked. Savey shook his head. "You never will. Come along."

Vance reached under his bunk and brought forth a key. The corridor was uninhabited. They walked towards the Lavatory past the laundry chute, and Vance unlocked a door that Savey had seen a thousand times without consideration. He was used to Vance producing strange keys. These conveniences had been handed down, at a price, from generation to generation. They enabled the successful bidder to roam at will (from midnight on, at least) through forbidden territory. Their ownership was the most tightly guarded secret of modern times.

Savey followed Vance and his flashlight up an unsuspected stairway, through a second door, into an airless space largely occupied by a circular tank. At the far side the flash revealed an alcove fitted with folding chairs and an old oil lamp which Vance lighted. Also, Savey saw a variety of ash trays, laden with smoked butts, and the air itself was heavy with dead smoke.

"We call it the Cellar, Save, because it's the attic—more confusing. This obstruction is the big tank that used to furnish water for the Lav. Have a drag?" He held out the cigarette he had lit.

Savey had begun and ended his smoking one day when he was twelve. He accepted Vance's weed, however, for he wished to atone for siding with Sid.

"Keep it," and Vance lit another. "This place is known and used by only nine guys at any time. That's why I had to wait to initiate you. Hinckle was shipped this morning—for good. Nobody else but the chosen nine can join until someone dies, graduates, or is careless."

Savey wanted to ask why he had been inducted into this coveted membership but hesitated in the hope that Vance would explain. "You saw where I keep my key. You'll be given Hinckle's when he can get it back to us. You know most of the guys—Hobe and Nicky and Bud and Andy—I'll give you the list. But never mention this place to them. I'll tell them you're a member. The incoming member throws a party. I'll tell you about that later. You won't have to smoke, for it's a place of freedom, though you'll find it sociable."

"But why me?" Savey had to ask.

"Why do you suppose?" Vance retorted darkly. "I can

trust you. That's most important. The other guys like you, except Ordley. And I wanted to thank you for helping out with Sid, even if we didn't pull it off."

Savey felt better. He had no intention of smoking, not much anyway, but it would help with his book, for this hide-away asked for bull sessions. "Thanks," he said.

Vance killed his butt and said, "Nobody's supposed to come here until after eleven. Getting back's too dangerous. Let's go."

Savey saw Vance open the door into the corridor with the utmost caginess. No one was around. They undressed in the dark and Savey climbed into his bunk. He knew by the creaking below that a hundred and seventy pounds of athlete, adventurer, and friend had sought repose. He, however, was wide-awake. He was thankful that Vance had forgiven him but wished he had shown his gratitude in some other way.

*　　*　　*　　*　　*

Colt's first move after his election to Council was to visit Master Blaik McClintock, faculty advisor. The McClintock home stood in a circle of hemlocks and spruces and was deftly run by Alison McClintock and overrun by two sons and two daughters. Blaik himself was a quiet, patient, subtly humorous man of forty, who could be as firm as granite when something came up to be firm about. There was nothing petty about him. He put Colt at ease immediately by saying, "Mrs. McClintock rules this house, as you've probably been told, and one of her ordinances is that no guest leaves without nourishment. Besides, I feel like a little ginger ale myself. What would you like?"

They settled with their glasses and some cake by the fire

and Blaik said, "Council, as you may know, is made up of the Student Body President, the Chief Proctor, two permanent members from each of the three upper classes and a rotating man for each semester from each class. These boys are usually responsible and hard-working and take their duties seriously. You'll see, in a session or two, how genuine an honor it is to be chosen for the job, and from what I hear of you, I believe that you'll have much to contribute."

"I'd like to prove you right," Colt said quietly. "What *is* the chief thing I must do?"

"A broad question. Let me relieve your mind. No gumshoe work is expected. No listening behind doors. No hunting down the desperate criminal who is ten minutes late to something or other. The newcomer to Council nurses the delusion that he must spy on his fellows, but nothing is farther from the truth. Council acts on data brought to its notice. That's enough, I may add. It's a curious thing, nearly everything serious is brought to Council's attention."

"That makes it different," Colt said with relief.

"As you have probably become aware, our scheme of education is founded on three amazing fallacies. One is that the American boy yearns to be instructed. Another, that he likes to be led in the paths of righteousness. Thirdly, that he looks up to us in charge of him with profound admiration and gratitude. Am I correct?"

Colt grinned. This man was all right. He was human. "Does Master Ike think like that?" he asked.

"He does. That's why Ironwood School is a going concern. Master Ike knows boys and girls and tempers his magisterial sternness with that knowledge. He knows that if you could put a boy in a kettle and boil him away, you'd find a residue of common sense at the bottom. It is that fundamental quality that Master Ike tries to reach without resorting to the kettle. And Council is his chief instrument. We don't believe in force. We persuade. We try to prevent. Only in extreme cases do we give up and send the incorrigible student to other pastures."

Colt's grin disappeared. "Council must take a lot of time."

"That's its chief failing," Blaik concurred. "My large temptation as observer and possible referee, is to kick things along. Some Monday night I'll be carried out screaming and put away. We circle around issues like so many turkey buzzards, maimed ones at that. It's our Student Body President's meat. Bill Ordley, I regret to tell you, has an interest in seeing that nothing gets done. I'm sure I'm not surprising you with this information."

Colt said, "Why do you put up with him?"

"Because Master Ike is teaching democracy here, Colt, and it's a worth-while experiment. One learns fastest through mistakes. If boys' end gets a bellyful of this mistake, it may elect an S.B.P. of a different caliber in May."

Colt looked at the man gazing into the fire to see if he suspected that Master Harty had passed on their secret to Master Blaik. But the Council advisor gave no sign. Colt was reassured by one thing. If the impossible happened and he should be elected, it would be valuable to have weekly contact with Blaik.

*　　*　　*　　*　　*

After the first meeting of the Boys' Council, Colt felt more reconciled to the hours involved. He had watched, listened, learned; and he came away with a clearer sense of the worthwhileness of life at Ironwood than he'd had. Certainly Council represented the best element in the dorm. The boys, he thought, had exercised the detective gift for smelling out character. They had elected the pick of the dorms, and in return the boys offered the best they had. Colt felt a new allegiance growing in him.

The test of it came two mornings later. Seniors and Juniors in good standing were allowed to study in their rooms. Blessed quiet reigned in the halls. So it came about that Colt was alone when he found the cigarette butts in the Lav. Somebody had dumped several dozen butts in a toilet and either had forgotten to flush it or had done so too hastily. So there they floated, a sodden mess, and confronted Colt with his first temptation.

He looked over his shoulder. No one was about. The easy course was to know nothing, report nothing. Boys were bound to experiment in all directions. As soon as they became men, they would be praised for wanting to. But educators nipped this praiseworthy urge in the bud. Hygiene was hoisted onto the level of the Ten Commandments which became twenty. Colt had become so accustomed to the smoking, profanity, tippling, boasting and vicious behavior of those unfortunate years with the Hi-Gunners, that Ironwood seemed innocence itself. But he was now a Council member, was expected to report situations that undermined the morale of the School, and the growing smoke nuisance was one. His integrity restrained him from disposing of the butts, and his common sense, nourished by his native canniness, told him to obtain a witness. At the same instant he heard footsteps.

"Got a minute, Savey?" Colt called and pointed into the toilet.

Savey peered and the blood rushed into his cheeks.

"You recognize them?" Colt asked.

"Hardly." Savey was trying to imply that he never smoked.

"I didn't mean that. Someday I may need a witness. How many butts do you estimate?"

"Thirty, forty. Shall I count them?" If he had smoked the lot, his cheeks couldn't have shrieked it louder.

"Please don't mention this." Colt flushed the toilet. "Was the smoking as general last year?"

"I-I wouldn't know. I mean I didn't know, last year, that anyone smoked. Master Ike was here, and Master Crawford, the old dean of boys."

Colt knew what Savey was not saying: that Master Henry Vanner was too inexperienced to detect the misdemeanors that went on behind the scenes. He ignored Savey's flush. He thought it possible that Savey's roommate had smoked thirty cigarettes in the last few days; but Vance would never have been careless about the disposal of the butts. He suspected that Savey's embarrassment came from his knowledge of Vance's habits, knowledge that he could not impart.

Colt went back to his room. He was puzzled by his inconsistency of sentiment. He liked Vance almost as much as he disliked Ordley. It lay beyond reason. He also liked Savey. However inexperienced, timid, possibly even weak Savey was, he was good at heart in the ways that Colt respected—generous, kind, gentle, hard-working, ambitious, brainy, sympathetic. Probably Master Harty knew what he was doing in boosting Savey up the Tree of Knowledge with Vance lending a hand from the lower branches. But it was going to hurt the innocent one. Colt sat down, but his head was less occupied with chemistry than with the educational values of sin and the high cost of tuition. The trouble was that, like the Hi-Gunners, it followed you. You could hardly ever shake it.

When Council next met, at 9:30 the following Monday, Colt's jaw had the firm set which indicated that he was about to do something against his inclination. Routine business took time. The Council members yawned, looked at the clock, stretched. They had had a day of classes, athletics, and an evening of study. But Colt forced himself to ignore the signs of ennui and said, "I know it's late, but I think we can no longer postpone the smoking issue."

"Why ?" Ordley interrupted. "The school was never freer of smokers."

"I disupte that," Colt said quietly.

"You would, of course," Ordley said sarcastically. "You weren't even here last year."

"Well, I was," Ian MacQuarrie said. "Colt's right. I see fellows going on weed walks after every meal."

Ordley ignored Ian and said to Colt, "Some parents don't mind if their sons smoke a little. They probably send some in. There's no way to stop that unless you open the mails."

"Ingenious but mistaken," Master Blaik observed. "Master Ike makes sure that parents understand why our rules against student smoking are so strict. No parent sends cigarettes, you may be sure, because no parent wants to get his son into trouble."

"Let Colt say what's on his mind," Bellman put in.

"I found about thirty butts in a toilet in the Boys' Lav," Colt told them. "Somebody was careless."

The Council members' faces expressed surprise, curiosity, amusement, or embarrassment. "What nonsense!" Ordley exclaimed. "The staff smokes. No boy would've been that careless, you can bet."

"He should know," Bellman whispered loud enough to carry.

"I asked Bagley if they could have been staff butts," Colt went on coolly. "He said the staff smoked in the kitchen and laundry and power house and in the staff house and on the grounds, but never in the dorms. There was a severe penalty for that. And why should they bother to carry the butts upstairs when they'd been disposing of them for years in other ways?"

"If this discussion's going on into the night, I move we adjourn and take it up next week," Ordley broke in. "Any second?"

Nobody spoke. Colt looked at Master Blaik. "I don't know what's done next. Is there a precedent?"

"Yes," Blaik said. "A situation has been disclosed, so it is Council's duty to investigate it. In a matter where the guilt may be more or less evenly distributed . . ." A laugh interrupted this humorous statement, ". . . Council may take the case directly to the student body. The Student Body President presents the official view. This is simple. The consensus of opinion is that smoking is harmful for athletes and others under voting age. It offers a bad example to youngsters and is an acknowledged fire hazard to buildings as old as ours. If a boy puts his personal indulgence ahead of the advantages we offer him here, he should go elsewhere. We are gradual about it. His punishment is progressively severe, until after four lapses he finds himself again in the bosom of his family. No one regards this unjust, not even the culprit. But our duty is preventive as well as punitive, and I suggest that Student Body President Ordley address Morning Assembly to this effect."

"Me?" Bill exclaimed, while the others tried to repress smiles.

"You or some member you choose to delegate."

The irony of Ordley exhorting the student body not to smoke was too poignant to risk, and Bill said, "I delegate Colt to do it. He brought the thing up."

"Isn't it better for a new member to keep quiet?" Colt asked.

"As a general thing, yes," Blaik replied. "But you can catch the interest by relating your first-hand discovery and the details of your talk with Bagley. You may also quote me verbatim, if you wish."

"I approve," Ian said and the others assented.

"I move we adjourn," Ordley said, and the motion was carried.

* * * * *

Savey woke, heard low voices, and wondered how late it was. Bill Ordley was talking to Vance and losing his temper, as Vance had probably planned. "But you've got to," Ordley repeated.

"You can't have it both ways," Vance said calmly.

Savey wondered what Ordley wanted both ways. But who didn't? Vance wanted to smuggle forbidden things and not be fired. Hobey wanted to be Student Body President and to enjoy himself illegally. Ordley wanted to be big man on campus and act small. What did he, Savery A. Miller want? Education à la Ironwood and education à la Vance. As well ask fire to heat and cool you at the same time as to reach for opposites with both hands.

Savey blushed again in the dark as he relived his encounter with Colt and the cigarette butts. He admired Colt and wanted Colt's approval. What would Colt have thought if he'd known that he, Savey of the spotless reputation, had dumped those butts in the can and forgot to flush it?

You couldn't keep your mind on two things simultaneously, either. He'd been thinking of Lola's surprise if she should smell smoke on his breath. He'd been thinking how decent it was of him to clean up the Cellar for Vance without Vance's knowing who did it. He'd sneaked the butts down to the Lav—and then forgot the important thing. He'd tried to lie to Colt with that deceitful "Hardly!" while telling himself he was not lying. Trying to have it two ways again. He was a mess. He'd better get hold of himself, or he'd turn into another Ordley.

Savey wished he could understand what was being said. Ordley was nervous. "Colt'll keep shoving his nose in until he tracks you down. He's that kind."

"Down to what?" Vance asked coolly. "You dump the butts?"

"No. Who did?"

Savey held his breath. If Vance ever discovered his criminal negligence so soon after initiating him into the Cellar crowd, awful things might happen.

"How do I know?" Vance retorted. "And I'm not asking. I might murder the guy. Now get this: my contract with Alcibiades commits me to taking $200 worth of his stuff a month. The weed's a necessary part of that. I'm not going to shut down because you've got cold feet about our ex-gangster. If worst comes to worst, I'll show him up. I could probably buy enough evidence from his gun-mates to put him in the can. Colt won't squawk."

Savey was tense and scared. Vance was probably bragging about his power. Power, Savey had learned, was Vance's ambition, his obsession. But you couldn't be sure about Vance. He was deeper, and darker, than you thought. Savey shivered, for if Colt should really be threatened, it would be up to him to take Colt's side. That meant telling what he knew, and *that* would mean ending Vance's life at Ironwood—and his own. Could he make that sacrifice? Savey couldn't, he knew. Yet the opportunity might be just around the corner, the test of his very manhood. But how could a man squeal on his partners in crime? He couldn't. Suddenly a new light shone. Was that why Vance had initiated him into the fateful secret of the Cellar? Golly, living could certainly seem intricate at midnight.

Almost at once Savey saw by the light on the ceiling that Ordley had opened the door. It closed. Vance came to his bunk and whispered, "Save, you awake?"

Savey gave no sign of consciousness.

*   *   *   *   *

Colt looked at the time: 2:15 A.M. and the chemistry notes still to go over. Then he must outline his speech to

116

Boys' Assembly. He had never addressed a crowd in his life. Nor would this be easy. "You certainly pay for your education," he thought.

A long rumbling sound overhead claimed his attention. "Not that!" he groaned. This was the signal for a riot. Some fool rolled the shot-put ball along the dorm floor in the dead of night in barbarian protest against some ruling, and the riot followed.

Colt hesitated. He should be asleep. He could be asleep. It was the duty of Ordley's proctors to herd the rioters back into their rooms. But the fact not to be dodged was that he wasn't asleep, and he was a Council member.

Colt looked at Steve and decided not to wake him. This was not his responsibility. The two floors acted on the caste system. A riot on the naturally riotous third floor inhabited by sophomores and freshmen was severely let alone by the wise juniors and seniors of the floor below. Colt, as Council member, had a dimly recognized right, but knew that he would be reviled for butting in.

When he reached the darkness of the top dorm, only slightly mitigated by faint all-night lights in the ceiling, Colt made out the rioters swarming at the far end of the hall, opposite Funny Maxton's room. So that was it! The long-threatened rebellion against Funny's keeping Sid out of basketball had broken out. The cries that Colt heard might have come from the basketball floor.

"Over here! Pass him to me."

"No running with the ball!"

"Dribble, you nut."

"We want a goal! We want a goal," shouted joyous throats.

"He don't bounce good!"

"Keep the ball moving. Shove it along, squad."

"What if he won't drop through the basket."

"Give him a shower."

"Yeah!" shouted hoarse voices. "To the showers with him!"

They were laughing, thank heaven! Colt realized. Funny'd suffer nothing worse than humiliation. Colt could just make out that the central mass, self-defeating in its clumsy pushing, was getting nowhere. The core of the mass, Funny in person, was being heaved by human billows. The embattled Britisher was fighting silently—not for blood, but to keep his head above water.

"That's enough!" Colt shouted. "Break it up, fellows."

"Who's that? Who's the guy?" voices called.

"It's Colt," sang out a boy at his elbow.

"Out of bounds! Out of bounds!" roared several.

"Lynch him!" cried a voice Colt recognized as Hobey's. Of course! Hobey was engineer of this riot.

"Grab Colt!" Hobey was yelling. Colt noticed that Hobey was not leading any attack on him, however.

"All right, fellows! You've had your fun. Break it up!"

Suddenly the lights came on full—Master Henry Vanner's move.

"Throw Colt downstairs. Take Funny to the showers!" Hobey commanded. "You taking orders from Colt?"

Colt charged into the crowd towards Funny. The two of them could help each other. Boys jumped on Colt's shoulders. Someone banged the back of his head and he saw stars. He felt someone clinging to his legs. Then he heard yells. "Sid!" "It's Sid himself!" "Hi, Sid! We're putting Funny on the List."

Their laughter at that was smashed into by Sid's bellow. "Let go of Master Cecil or I'll break your necks."

"But we're taking you off the List," came Hobey's voice.

"I'm *off* the List!" roared Sid. "Let go of Funny."

Colt freed himself from the clutch of hands and shouldered his way to Funny as Sid reached him. "Too bad, sir," Sid said to Funny. "You hurt?"

"Thanks . . . no." Funny was panting, his pajama jacket was in streamers, the sweat glistened on a face that managed a smile.

"This wouldn't have happened if you'd let me tell them," Sid said.

Reinforcements were arriving. Henry Vanner had Ian MacQuarrie, Steve Livey and half a dozen seniors in his wake. The rioters melted back into their rooms with exemplary promptness. In fifty seconds only the guiltless remained.

Colt gazed at Sid in unspoken admiration. Master Henry was asking Funny some questions. "The third floor will offer you a formal apology in the morning, Cecil."

"It's the last thing I want," Funny protested.

"Wouldn't it be better if Council handled this?" Ian asked the dean of boys.

"Somebody's got to straighten it out," Sid said. "Master Cecil's been tutoring me for a week and I'm off the List. I can play tomorrow."

"So the riot's irony," Colt said. "Sid, you've got your illustration for all the exams to come."

"Just when Master Cecil says he's going to drop that question," Sid said with a grin. "Would that be irony, too?"

"It's after two o'clock," Henry Vanner reminded them. "Ian, I'll speak to Master Harty before breakfast as to how this affair's to be handled. Go get your sleep."

"May I speak to Colt for a moment?" Funny asked.

Vanner nodded and took the others with him. Colt followed Funny into his room. With the door shut, Funny said, "I'll make it short, for you must be tired. First, thanks for the happy ending. You got me out of a ducking. I don't know what's ahead, but without your quick assistance, it would have been worse."

"Nothing will happen. They'll feel a bit sheepish in your presence for a day or two."

"I didn't mean about me, but about the List. Sid could easily slide back onto it, you know."

"It won't be the same. Your tutoring Sid and getting him off has changed things. They jumped you because they thought you didn't care."

"Sid begged me to let him tell them. I thought it was a matter between us two. I'll never get on to the American way of thinking."

"You'll have their respect now," Colt said.

"Now what can I do for you?" Funny asked. "They have it in for you for coming to my rescue."

"I'll survive," Colt said. "It's out of their systems."

"Do you know," Funny said suddenly. "I feel that. I think things will be different. In spite of the riot, I'm happier

120

this moment than at any time since I hit Ironwood, as you say."

"Good," Colt said and meant it. For the first time since Funny's coming he felt really friendly to the man.

*　　*　　*　　*　　*

Colt's sleep was ravaged by nightmares of rioters and his tongue-tied efforts to talk sense into them. Sounds of hurried footsteps past his door woke him. He lay there, without will, saying to himself that he must think out his speech to Assembly, but knowing that the real reason for skipping breakfast was to avoid mingling with the boys. For anything might happen if Hobey chose to incite them.

Steve roused him from his half-doze by bringing in a teapot and toast.

"Where did you dig that up?" Colt asked.

"You've got more friends than you think," was all that Steve would say, since a Council Member was happier when he did not hear of fractured rules. Hot plates were forbidden because of the fire hazard. So Vance naturally kept one, as a man needed something hot when he came in damp and cold from an illicit errand. Savey had done without breakfast and risked Vance's wrath by brewing support for Vance's rival.

Colt's dressing was interrupted by a summons to Master Harty's office brought by Ian MacQuarrie.

Morning Assembly opened daily with a Bible reading selected and given by the boys in rotation, followed by announcements and dismissal to classes. This routine, too short for sleep, too ordinary for interest, was accepted in the same spirit as when one dressed, that is, with one's mind on something else.

This morning of expectation the hundred and fifty boys were tense. Retribution could take one of several different shapes. They scanned the platform for portents of the immediate future. Usually the boy-of-the-day Bible reader and the Student Body President were the only platform-sitters. On this day of omen Bill Ordley presided and Willie Waters sat behind the stand with the Bible on it; that was all.

The doors closed. Then Waters stepped to the desk. A boy was permitted to select any portion of the Scriptures he pleased. To Colt this moment was a perpetual detective story; it told so much about the boy. The privilege was treated seriously; and for this reason the boys listened.

Lily Waters, as the self-effacing reader had been christened two years before, was an unknown. His shyness had developed a protective conduct that enabled him to slide through the weeks practically invisible. Colt was curious to see if he would choose a passage equally colorless. Lily opened his mouth, but no sound came, tried again and announced "First Kings, Chapter 3, verses 16 to 28."

Colt sat straighter. This turned out to be the story of Solomon's decision as to which of the two women was the mother of the child that both claimed. And Lily was reading it well. The hands holding the Bible trembled, his voice didn't. And suddenly Colt was aware of tension in his throat. This was the unappreciated boy's bid for justice. When he finished, the living silence told Colt that the boys were impressed. They had expected the ludicrous and had been moved by Lily's measuring up to the occasion. Then a second illumination swept

122

Colt: perhaps Lily was calling for justice to be done to Funny Maxton, too. Maybe the kid was deep. Then he saw Bill Ordley rise. The Student Body President, usually so brazenly confident, looked fussed. "Colt Muir has an announcement to make for Council," he said lamely and sat down.

Colt, being tall, sat in the back of the room. He felt the hostile silence as he walked forward to the platform. Lily Waters' example braced him. Surely he must not show his nervousness after that boy's fine evidence of self-control.

"Two announcements, but short," he said. "One painful, one pleasant." His eye for some reason happened to single out Neil MacQuarrie's maturing face, watching him expectantly.

"Master Isaac Ironwood rules out smoking by the student body, for health reasons, and because a fire here might sweep the building before all could get out. I happened to find thirty cigarette butts in one of the Lav toilets. I interviewed enough of the staff to be convinced they were students' butts. By agreement I had to notify Council and Council has to take note. We are a democracy here and the fundamental principle of a democracy is equal rights for all. Master Ike believes in democracy enough to give us lots of rope. He also believes that in a serious matter like this, we'll live up to the democratic principle. If someone doesn't, if some boy puts his own pleasure ahead of the public good, he is liable to the well-known consequences. Council has asked me to notify you that smoking must stop. The rules will be enforced."

Colt paused. The boys sat stolid, disappointed. They had come keyed up to hear what would be done because of the riot. Colt felt their mood, but dare not let himself be shaken.

"Now for the other announcement. Some years ago we

123

licked Master Cecil Maxton's King George the Third for the sake of the democratic principle. We've forgotten something, I'm afraid. For last night the rioters tried to lick Master Cecil for sticking up for *his* principles. There was no justice in it. Bill Waters has just shown you how impressive, how necessary justice is, if the world's not to go sour.

"Here are the facts: Master Cecil has spent his free time tutoring Sid Dalton off the List. He would not let Sid tell this, lest it raise false hopes. Now Master Cecil has asked Master Harty not to punish the third floor's hot heads. And since Master Cecil is a very stubborn Britisher, Master Harty gives in. I suggest that, if you feel like accepting Master Cecil's terms, you give three salvos to him."

A hundred and fifty voices, always ready for a noise, gave the famous Ironwood cheer of approval in a manner that showed the slate wiped clean.

Colt remained standing. "Master Harty wishes to add a word."

The now happily wrought up boys applauded the popular Harty who took Colt's place on the platform and said, "Sometimes it takes a thunderstorm to clear the air. One doesn't punish thunderstorms. The sun comes out and we start again. But we aren't as before. We are refreshed.

"Let me refresh your minds with some history that isn't in the books. As you know, the famous, or rather the infamous List is an old Ironwood institution. We thought it worked pretty well. But our new master from Oxford questioned the automatic functioning of the List. In reality we did, too, for we were easing up on students who sank below the notorious average of 60, when we thought occasion warranted.

124

"Came this Britisher, with his stubborn, but clear-headed stand for scholarship, no matter how athletic the student might be. He was good enough not to question our honesty, but he did insist on our thinking out the situation again. This we have done this morning, and I am delegated to report that the automatic List has been abolished."

The roar greeting this astonishing statement must have been heard at girls' end. It took minutes to quiet it. Then Harty continued. "Don't get your hopes up. We are starting a trial of individual cases, each case on its own merits. Our standards remain as before. If a boy of known character is laboring under an English deficiency, let us say, he will be labored with on his own merits. I believe that Master Ike will sanction this amendment of discipline. But it is up to you boys—and the girls—to prove that the new system is practicable in the months of school remaining. If it makes life rosier for you, you have Master Cecil's stand on principle to thank for it. Now we're late, so please go at once to your classrooms."

The Assembly scattered with loud words of joy and happy faces. But Vance was not one of the jubilant. He edged over to Hobey and said, "Why did Ordley give Colt that chance to talk? It was Ordley's place. He's just handed Colt a bunch of votes. Last night handed him votes. I'd like to know who left those butts in the can. Now we've got to cut out bringing in the weed for a while. And will Mr. Smith be sore!"

10 -
The Electrocution Contest

State Senator Alonzo Griggson, a graduate of Ironwood School in 1886, had provided for "An Elocution Contest" as he termed it, because he believed in good blood going in for political careers. Public duty involved dignified debate, and he wished to encourage public speaking. Hence his generous award.

In accordance with his rules, Acting Headmaster Harty read the conditions in Boys' Assembly on March 1st, as follows:

"As the old record put it, no boy who chews tobacco or keeps gaming cocks is eligible. No relative of the donor is eligible. Only one prize is awarded. The subject of the speech must be dear to the speaker's heart. The speech may be prepared or be impromptu, in which case the subject will be supplied by the three judges. These men are to be the headmaster, the senior English master, and a member of the State Legislature. They will judge the speaker on his clarity, forcefulness,

126

persuasiveness, steadiness of delivery, and the ability to move his hearers. The prize: $250 for a prepared speech, $500, if impromptu."

On previous years Savey Miller had listened to this announcement with complete detachment, as if it concerned the beheading of Charles I of England. Savey knew it was not for him. Since the slightest hint that he might have to subject himself to the public gaze threw him into a fever of self-consciousness, he left public office to others. Somebody else could be President of the United States.

On this blowy day of March, however, Savey listened with horrified attention. He *must* have money, and a lot of it, or his nearly finished book could never appear. Inquiries as to the cost of getting it published appalled him. The lowest bid was $325 for 500 copies. If, as he dared to hope, the book could be put on sale at other boarding schools, the costs would mount.

Yet he *must* see this child of his in print. He had come to love it, and laughed heartily at its wit when no one else was in the Library. He yearned for the fame it would bring the unnamed author—for he could not scandalize his mother by publishing it over his name. He wished he could have dedicated it to Vance openly, instead of "To One Who Helped." At least he would have the joy of seeing boys actually reading his book and overhearing comments that would certainly be frank if nothing else.

And now the Contest dangled the means of achieving his desire before his anguished gaze. As he listened to the familiar rules, a cold shiver ran up and down his spine, like a ghost practising scales. The doubled value of the impromptu speech also doubled the agony beyond endurance. It was bad enough to mount the platform in full view of hundreds, and worse to open his mouth to utter words. But at least the words would be carefully memorized and he had a dependable memory. Not to have the words already stored—to speak on some subject given by the judges—would be impossible. He froze now in his seat at the thought. Yet the money!

In past years, Savey recollected, few had chosen to speak impromptu. And they had been almost invariably unequal to producing anything half as good as the orators who were secure in polished preparation. Yet last year, Pete Jeffers had boldly replied, "Impromptu" when Master Ike asked, and Savey remembered his own nervousness, safe as he was in his chair, for Pete. It was wasted sympathy. Pete's face was a help. It was droll before he spoke. The judges offered as subject "The Day I Came to School."

Pete had been inspired to build up a story of his apprehensions. Then, on the fateful day, he had simply walked into the school. The walls didn't fall on him. Nobody in the faculty bit him. He was too inconspicuous for the Committee on Initiation to notice. Pete soon reduced his audience to quivering jellies—and got the $500. But Savey knew that he couldn't be funny, intentionally, if beheading were the alternative.

Master Harty closed with a few words of encouragement, and Savey made a vow. He would compromise. He would give a prepared speech, trusting to luck that no one else would go impromptu. He would make it so certainly a winner that the $250 would be his. Perhaps then he could borrow the rest and pay it back from profits.

Vance caught up to him on their way to class. "You're entering?"

Savey nodded. "It's a secret."

"Impromptu, of course."

"I couldn't."

Vance frowned. "You want the money?"

"That's why I enter at all."

"Remember last year? Harvey Jenkins boning up on the social customs of Borneo, head-hunters and all that? Then Pete Jeffers came in, slick as hair oil, just saying things that every boy went through, and Harvey didn't have a chance."

"Mostly nobody goes impromptu," Savey said desperately.

" 'Mostly's' no insurance."

Bellman joined them and said to Vance, "You're entering?"

"Me?" Vance grinned. "Not on your life. I like my chewing tobacco and gaming cocks too much."

Bellman did not even ask Savey, whose shyness was well known. He and Vance moved on and left Savey in a stew of rebellion, ambition, doubts, and other thoughts which were worse than unhappy.

*   *   *   *   *

Savey seated himself for the three-dozenth time in the Library with *The Industrial Revolution* propped before him as a screen. But this time was different. The work was done. The manuscript, which had cost him the concentration of his

129

life and reduced his classroom standing, lay in its final form before him. He had torn up enough foolscap to run a paper chase. But now the only task remaining was to decide on a title and make small revisions.

Teacher Lola had watched the new Savey for weeks, the uncommunicative, and no longer shy boy, who worked steadily and almost secretively. The assistant librarian was not devoid of curiosity. She had become resigned to Savey's transfer of interest to Cornelia Craig. It was better so, although his brown head with the slightly curly hair, his straight serious nose, and the curve of his lengthening cheek still appealed to her. She could not bear to hear nothing of his problems. Certainly he must be floored by something most unusual. If only he would confide in her, as he used to do, she might help.

Savey had noticed Lola's solicitude but wanted none of it. If he dare not let Vance know what he was doing, he certainly could not give her the merest hint. As with most girls he had met, Lola loved to express her thoughts, and other people's. The fact that talk was barred in the Library made it twice as necessary elsewhere.

Savey consulted the list of possible titles he had been jotting down for weeks. ANYBODY WANT A GIRL? . . . GIRLS WITHIN REACH OF ALL . . . A GUIDE TO GIRLS . . . WE TELL YOU HOW . . . FORTY WAYS TO WOO AND WIN . . .

They all had promise and need not be wasted, for he could use them as chapter-heads. But which had the quickest salespower? He wished he could consult Vance or Hobey. They'd know instantly. He decided to postpone the choice of title and read his introduction:

START HERE

Fellows, here it is at last! The first schoolboy guide to dating. The inside dope to what you want. The book of knowledge.

What's your happiness worth to you? Before you get red-faced, tongue-tied, and miss the bus, consult the index to this manual and locate your trouble. Then learn the way out.

Boys, throw that wishbone away and bungle no more evenings. We pass on to you our hard-won technique so that you need have no more embarrassing moments. We guarantee to wipe out that shyness and boost you on top of the world that counts.

One warning. *Do not lend this handbook.* It's the only practical revelation of its subject to be offered high school undergrads. After one reading, any tow-headed, freckle-faced, bandy-legged, cock-eyed freshman will be able to annex the girl of his fancy. But keep this golden wisdom to yourself. The more you give these secrets away, the harder the competition. Read, then *confidently* do your stuff, for WE TELL YOU HOW.

Savey frowned, for he had become a stern self-critic. This preface was too wordy and repetitious. He drew a line of disapproval through the long words that classic literature had provided. It had been difficult to downgrade his vocabulary from *Hamlet* to Hobey. And how painful to leave out the picturesque directness of bull session speech! When would the world grow up and no longer need to be shielded from its children's conversations?

Savey turned to

Chapter One. HOW TO BEGIN

You spot a girl in the hall, on the dance floor, across the gameroom. She looks neat, smooth, cool. You have that feeling, and would like to date her for the Saturday Evening Program. You take steps—and are given the air. What was wrong?

It must have been something about you. Either you made a sour impression or none at all. She liked little about you and wanted it as far off as possible. *Why?* Friend, that is your question. *Why?*

Let's begin with your surface and work in. Girls today demand style. They love luster, however disguised in informality. A guy must shine in one of the accepted ways. So make tracks to the nearest mirror and look. You may, scholastically, be as bright as the mental power-houses who make *Cum Laude,* but if you resemble a moulting dromedary, you'll not get to first base. No girl wants to be a camel-herder.

Mirrors are rude; they point. But they are best friend to the earnest dater. Make the inspection honest. Then, after you've washed up cleaner than your mother ever made you, pressed the trou, taught your hair its place, and shown TASTE in tie, socks, shirt—and remember, a shirt is only spotless once—you may be set. Or nearly.

Nearly? Well, half. For the precision dater, the guy

who combines know-how with what it takes, has found that a wow wears off. It's what's underneath the polish that counts most. He has to dress and comb his state of mind—off stage, at that. He . . .

Savey became conscious of footfalls. Teacher Lola was straightening magazines and brushing shelf-edges with her feather duster. He wondered why he had ever let the assistant librarian put him through the wringer. Then he started with inspiration. He could add her to the varieties of girls explained in Chapter Nine. THE FEATHER DUSTER. That was better than Hobey's name for her, "Little Iceberg." Icebergs had weight.

He made a note and saw that Lola was moving in on him. He turned the incriminating pages face down and tried to look unconcerned. He *felt* guilty, in spite of Vance's training. He had spent valuable time concocting trouble for the faculty. Daters would certainly try to apply his instructions to their needs and increase the necessity of supervision by Teacher Minnie and her kind. Lola was only three strides away. Savey drew *The Industrial Revolution* closer.

Dissimulation had become exhilarating, if not easy, in such moments of danger. If Lola knew how he had used her during his weeks of dissecting femininity on paper, she would be outraged. She had posed for his imagination as a prude, a high-brow, an heiress; as the vain girl, the silly, the shallow, the stubborn, the dumb. In each case he had plotted the way around her to victory à la Vance. Lola was defenseless through all this, as defenseless as ever a girl was—in a book. So now

Savey was not disposed to flee but to try his own mastery of his instructions. She reached him.

"Dear me, Savery," came that light voice that had once rendered him breathless. "What *can* be giving you all this trouble lately?"

Savey touched *The Industrial Revolution* to imply his difficulty. His attention was suffused by a faint perfume, the merest arbutus-like hint of it. Ten weeks ago it would have evaded his consciousness; now he inhaled with delight. Vance, one might say, had practically created Savey's sense of smell. He made a mental addition to Chapter Sixteen, GIRL VALUES.

"If it's so hard for you, I don't see what will happen to the rest of the class. I really don't." Lola flicked at the area within an inch of the telltale pages, but got nothing, and went on. Presently Savey resumed the correction of his work:

Chapter Two. CONSTRUCTING CONFIDENCE.

Suppose you are given the chance of playing a solo at the Music Club concert, or of entering the Elocution Contest for big money? Will you back out and lose your opportunity to impress girls' end because you lack—the word is guts. Suppose you must address the Autumn Get-Together, or Vespers, or even a prospective date? What must you have? Technique, more widely called Know-How, *and* Confidence.

Confidence is to success what air is to lungs, the first necessity. And what is Confidence in dating? It is the unshakeable belief that girl needs boy as much as boy wants girl. It is the state of mind built on the undeniable proposition that no fellow is unwelcome to a girl unless a more attractive male is within reach. Therefore the solution to this basic problem is simply to be the most attractive guy in any given situation.

Is this difficult? Very. Is it impossible? Never. Enter Technique . . .

A sudden blast of icy air scattered Savey's pages in a dozen directions. Teacher Lola had opened the west window. Savey cursed under his breath, but not far under.

"Oh Savery!" Lola cried contritely. "I'm *so* sorry. I didn't realize it was so windy. Can you forgive me?" She hurried towards him.

"Please don't bother," Savey said in his effort to pick all the pages up simultaneously.

"Of course I shall. I've caused you all this trouble."

"I wish you wouldn't," Savey retorted gruffly.

"But there are so many of them!" Lola stooped.

"*Don't!*" The note of command sounded strange even to himself.

Lola hesitated, straightened up, and handed him the pages she had grasped. "Of course, if you prefer," she said coolly. She seemed rather flushed from stooping.

Savey took the pages without further word and Lola withdrew. He noticed that several pages were face up. Worst of all, the chapter heading HOW TO WOO AN ICEBERG was brutally visible. He had no intention of keeping that title. He had used it merely as reminder of the reference to Lola.

Savey cursed again.

*　　*　　*　　*　　*

Neil MacQuarrie, the born countryman, loved snow: it was such excellent fertilizer and waterbank. Other, subtler influences pulled him forth into a snowstorm. When the fall was heavy and drifting, Neil was as restless as a fish on a bank. He wished to submerge in his native element.

Scupper Riley disliked snow. It required distressing circumstances to fall, that is, cold weather. Scupper had been born thin, and nature had pulled him out thinner to get him longer. So he hated cold next to the infrequency of meals. Warmth and food were heaven; cold and starvation were otherwise, and Scupper avoided them.

When food and cold tugged in different directions Scupper was perplexed. It had required Neil's allying himself with food to induce Scupper to risk frostbite and detentions for the supreme adventure: a meal at the Café Alcibiades. Neither boy had ventured inside this forbidden portal, and complete manhood depended on daring this step upward. Snow afforded the safest screen from censorious eyes.

The storm had gained a gratifying intensity by nine that night. After a careful scouting, Neil and Scupper faded out of a basement window near a vast spruce tree that had been concealing exits for generations. The mile, mostly downhill, excited the appetite, and the boys stomped into the dimly lighted joint, whitened images of Hunger.

It was a slow evening at the Greek's, and Alcibiades served hoagies and hot chocolate with a malicious joy at being able to render a disservice to the hated rulers of Ironwood School. He preferred older customers; they chattered less and spent more. But he had seen few hungrier than these two.

There was another guest in the kitchen. Suddenly his

136

raised voice became recognizable. "Double it . . . Yep, I said it . . . You'll get your money . . . You always have, haven't you? . . . Tomorrow, sure . . . All right, all right . . . And hurry it. I'll get you know what if I'm late for lights out."

"Nicky!" Scupper said.

"We're going to slide," Neil whispered.

"We haven't had the pie."

"Sshh!" Neil nodded to the kitchen.

Nicky sounded aggrieved. "I know, I know, it's big money . . . Sixty-two fifty . . . He can read. You'll have it tomorrow."

"Come on hijacker, we're going to have fun." Neil rose.

"We've got to pay and don't know . . ."

"Leave that to me and slap into your coat."

They heard a door slam. Neil counted out the cost and added half a dollar to the pile of change. The Greek's ear was attuned to the ring of silver and he looked in. "You no want pie?"

"They lock the doors early when it snows," Neil said with a straight face. "See you again soon." Then he dove into his coat.

Alcibiades was a fast thinker but not so fast a mover as his animated guests. Neil was out first and led Scupper around to the back door. Nicky's trail was easy to follow if you bent into the choking flow of flakes which seemed to bring a dim illumination with them. "Don't talk," Neil commanded. "We'll let him carry the stuff up the hill for us and jump him at the door."

Scupper had no breath to talk. Neil, who had eaten less,

set a painful pace, for they had to circle ahead in order to intercept their quarry. Nicky's legs were shorter and he carried the pack. They accomplished the detour and found no fresh tracks at the probable entrance. Lights from a hundred windows threw radiance into the fleecy night. At length they made out a figure making for the sportsroom door. But it carried no pack.

"Foiled!" Scupper whispered. "And we missed the pie."

"He's left it somewhere. Come." Neil began backtracking along Nicky's trail and soon found it curving to the ancient spruce under whose branches they had made their getaway. Neil ducked under and stumbled on Nicky's pack. "So that's it," he said. "He's going to wait till lights out. What shall we do? We could hide it up the tree. Boy, Nicky'll blow his top."

"Where'd he get sixty-two bucks?" Scupper asked.

"He's got big shots behind him," Neil said. "Vance or Ordley. I hope it's Ordley who's going to worry. Only a stinker would crum in stuff and be Student Body President at the same time. I don't wonder Colt's mad."

"Vance is no angel," Scupper commented.

"No, but he isn't one in a nice way. There's no meanness in him. I'm for helping Colt, without turning anybody in."

"That's right. Our faces aren't so clean."

Neil laughed. "You hand me the pack and I can lodge it up in the boughs. They'll never look, for they'd never suppose the guy who found it would leave it."

Neil started up and Scupper execrated him for dislodging snow down his neck. Scupper lifted the heavy pack with a groan. Neil balanced it well up but a gust of wind nudged it

138

loose. The pack bounced and fell and burst open, revealing its treasure. At the same moment the lights went out. A basement window squeaked open and a flashlight uncovered Scupper bending over a pile of forbidden merchandise. Vance quietly commanded him to stand still or be shot. Scupper was not afraid of gunfire, but he had no intention of deserting Neil.

Vance reached him and said, "So you've taken to highway robbery. Don't you know it's a jail offense? You and Neil were crumming to Alcibiades. You'd better keep your faces shut about this. Where's Neil?"

Vance was answered by Neil in person, slithering from above and bearing Vance with him onto the snowy ground. Vance struggled, but Scupper pinned him down. Neil rubbed snow into his face for good measure, when Scupper said, "Sshh! Someone's signaling."

Vance had timed his exit to coincide with lights out without counting on extended operations outdoors. Bagley, the night watchman, began his rounds at boys' end and in the basement where an unlatched window might mean crummers afoot. Now he climbed out of the window and thrust his lantern in the dripping faces. "So it's you," he said gruffly to his three prizes. "Get up. And bring your stuff. Council's sitting and would like to see this."

There was no alternative, no dodging Bagley the incorruptible. They brushed, rubbed, shook, and scraped the snow from them in silence. A pity about Vance, Neil thought. He was a good guy, in a way, and the school would miss him, in basketball anyway. A thousand pities it hadn't been Ordley. Vance looked sober and rather handsome in the lanternlight,

Neil realized. Good soft-hearted Neil was for the underdog—to a point. He was sure that Vance wouldn't squeal on his and Scupper's crum to the Greek's.

"Come along now, and no breaking away," Bagley ordered. "March ahead of me with that stuff."

*　　*　　*　　*　　*

The very breeze in a school carries the news, and Hobey Tyler crept down sleepily before breakfast for a secret parley with his partner. He sat on the edge of Vance's bunk. "What happened?"

"Neil and Scup loused it up. Bags caught me with the goods. Council made it snappy. I get two weeks vacation at home. Don't ride Neil or Scupper. They didn't let on Nicky was in it. They'd been crumming to Alcibiades' and weren't in a position to talk."

"How about me?"

"You weren't mentioned."

"Want me to tell Harty I'm in it too?"

"For gosh sake *no!* You're staying here to quiet Alcibiades and the Student Body President. The school's holding the stuff, and Alcibiades will be yelling for his sixty bucks. Maybe you can borrow a down payment and stuff it into his mouth, or he'll get nasty."

"I'll tell him you'll bring it back with you. Any chance of getting a job for the two weeks?"

"Out of character," Vance said. "I'd have to explain to the folks. They'd shove me into Broughtonville High. No thanks. I want my Ginny."

"I'll bet she could raise that cash for you."

"Leave Ginny out of this," Vance said hoarsely. "One

thing you can do and that's cut Ordley's throat. Gosh, I'd hate his guts, if he had any. What do you think he said after he had sentenced me—imagine *him* sentencing me—after we'd left the Council room, he said, 'Now you can bring back the forty bucks you owe me.' His one thought. And you should've heard his pure and lofty tone while conducting the investigation. You might suppose he'd never done anything fancy in his life, the darned smug hypocrite! Hobe, I respect you for offering to cut in on this, but it'd be a waste of piety. Save it. You've *got* to make S.B.P. now."

"Do you really think your parents will take you out of school?"

"I don't mind facing Dad, who chased around a bit himself, I gather. But Mom'll look bad and say 'I was so proud of you.' It certainly is a problem, bringing up parents. Now cut back to your room, Hobe, and be good. I leave after breakfast."

"I'll keep Alcibiades quiet, Vance. Be seeing you."

The door closed and Vance said, "You awake, Save?"

"I didn't hear a thing," Savey said with a low laugh.

"Good boy, if you can help Hobe find a little cash, I'd appreciate it."

11 -

Up to Easter Vacation

A cloudless sky greeted the arisers as if nature had turned over a new leaf, as Master Harty advised the departing Vance to do. The same afternoon Colt carried the bundle of cigarette cartons down to Alcibiades' joint.

Harty and Blaik McClintock had decided that Council had better manage this situation. The school could threaten legal procedure, but Isaac Ironwood's policy was to enforce democracy at home rather than call in the law. The boys and girls would always be confronted by temptation; the thing was to train them to make right choices.

So Council, on Ian MacQuarrie's motion, delegated Colt to restore Vance's purchases and see that the $62.50 was canceled on the Greek's books. A warning was to be added.

Colt was not averse to the errand. He had heard enough about this outlaw and he was glad to have a hand in subduing Ironwood's No. 1 enemy. He carried the bundle around to the back door and knocked. The door opened an inch, then a

142

foot, and the dark-skinned proprietor asked what the new-comer wanted.

"A business matter, Mr. Alcibiades. You've got your best customer sent home from school."

"Who're you?"

"A classmate of Vance Draper's, Colton Muir."

Alcibiades stiffened and Colt expected the door to slam in his face. But the little chisel-cold eyes glinted with another idea. "Come in, we talk." Colt was led through the kitchen, past storerooms, to a small private dining room. He set his bundle on a table and opened it.

"The school's Council returns this. I want a receipt showing that you've received it and have taken the $62.50 charge off your books."

The Greek's features tightened. "He bought, he pay. They not mine."

"Do you want angry parents demanding that the school close you up for selling cigarettes to minors?"

The joint keeper had not grown rich by flinching before threats. He rose and said angrily, "I know you now. You one of Hi-Gunners gang. You go round shaking down poor man like me. You get out here quick or you be sorry, much."

Colt rose in order not to be taken at a disadvantage. He watched carefully, as in the old days, for a hand's movement to the hip. "You're wrong. I'm no Hi-Gunner."

"I know all about you. Vance show me the newspaper. You put big fellow in jail, Red Mahovey."

"You didn't read enough," Colt said. "I once belonged to a street club named Hi-Gunners. When gangsters moved in and spoiled it, I left. They didn't like that and sent Red

143

Mahovey to get me, and he did. He had me tied up to be secretly put out of the way. But a friend of mine notified the State Police and rescued me. Do you understand what I'm saying?"

"That's how you tell it. I like hear Red Mahovey tell it."

Colt produced a paper. "This is a statement from Council," he explained. "It pledges you to stop selling your wares to Ironwood students and to refuse them as customers. If you do not sign it, Council advises the school to take legal action."

"I read." A sinewy hand reached for the typed statement. The man was slow, Colt thought, at taking in a simple order.

"Who this Council? You?"

"I'm one of twelve boys with a faculty advisor. Now please sign and add that you have canceled the $62.50 order."

To Colt's hidden amazement, Alcibiades unclipped a pen from his flannel shirt pocket and signed. Colt knew that his kind did not defeat easily. His acquiescence was too quick. But it was not the time or place to try to guess what guile might lurk behind the action. "You have a drink—like old time, eh?" Alcibiades asked suddenly with a rather curious smile.

Colt's wits were challenged to instant action. Ought he to refuse the proffered hospitality or stay and try to see behind that furrowed brow? "Thanks, yes. Ginger ale, if you have some."

"Boys' drink," Alcibiades said with a leer. "You man, now, plenty tough."

"I'd like a drink of ginger ale. In the bottle," he added, as a precaution against a doped drink.

Twenty minutes later Colt had to admit that he knew

little more. But at least he was taking back the receipt. He thanked Alcibiades and left. The Greek stared after him deep in thought.

*   *   *   *   *

Savey was shocked by Vance's disclosures. He had guessed, of course, that something was going on, perhaps more gambling, or crumming to Alcibiades' during faculty meetings. But he hated to learn that Vance had helped the Greek degrade the dorms and had got Nicky, who hadn't half Vance's brains, into trouble. Nicky had looked sadly sober as he left for his fortnight's retirement.

Yet there was something about Vance that kept Savey from agreeing with Teacher Lola that Vance did nothing but breed trouble and should be expelled. Vance wanted to get on and was having a hard time finding his way. His secret daring, his masculine urge for mastery, attracted Savey. Vance had rescued him from the nursery and Savey was grateful.

Savey understood the wrath of Coach Kress and the basketball team. "A swell Ironwoodian!" Ian exploded in the lockerroom. "This is the second time he's let this team down." And down the team went, though battling desperately under Sid Dalton's leadership. The maddening score, 49 to 52, could have been reversed with Vance, although Westtown offered no weakness to take hold of. Savey had promised to write Vance about the game. He omitted Kress's remarks on Vance's absence, which had turned the Kress temper into a blowtorch that burned with little sound.

However, he could quote from Master Harty's speech in joint Assembly. Harty said, "If determination is praiseworthy, if the courage to come up behind is a moral quality, then we

145

need not be utterly gloomy. The magnificent efforts of Dalton, Bellman, MacQuarrie, Tyler, and Evans, who was subbing for Vance Draper, did miracles against a Westtown team who had no right to be so peerless. Finally, we have one recourse against this haughty school—the baseball game in May. Coach Kress's hand has been stayed from suicide by the hope of winning that game. Let me add the faculty's humble vote of thanks for the gallant endeavor on the basketball team's part. Now let's have three salvos for the victorious vanquished."

Savey missed Vance, but did catch up on a lot of sleep, and Vance could not nag him into going impromptu in the Elocution Contest. He had written a speech about an Indian boy's coming of age. Steve Livey supplied him with data about the Blackfoot Indians, whose reservation in Alberta he had visited. Savey made a dramatic account of the rigors that a young Indian had to endure before the men of his tribe recognized him as a man. He brought the whole subject upstage by entitling his speech "The Conditions of Self-Respect."

In Savey's opinion, the genius who had tagged Senator Griggson's spectacle The Electrocution Contest was a realist. As the day neared—a week away, two days away, *tomorrow*— he would have preferred the electric chair. *That* was all over in a few seconds, while his Indian boy took eight minutes. His only stay against nervousness was his determination to be letter-perfect, phrase-perfect, intonation steady, stance moderately aggressive, and his gestures vivid.

The day dawned cloudy and cold. Luncheon tasted like pencil shavings and excelsior. Savey stole outdoors to take his mind off the approaching horror and rehearse his speech. He headed for the woods beyond the Village where no one would intrude. As he passed Alcibiades' hangout, he heard a dog's howls and saw some of the Village toughs shying chunks of ice at the mongrel. The dog had fled up a dead-end alley and could escape only by charging into them.

Savey was tempted to intervene for the pooch's sake, but the odds were too big, especially as Ironwoodians were hated bloodily by the Village gangs. So Savey sped on, not happy about his common sense. When did common sense turn into cowardice? What would his Indian boy have done? Was he living up to his own conditions of self-respect? Would Vance have saved his skin in this way? Honestly, no.

Suddenly a brilliant idea stopped Savey cold. He'd go back, rescue the dog from the bullies' punishment, and restore his self-respect. He might get roughed up so badly that he could not appear in the Contest. But that way out was also cowardice. He hadn't entered the Contest to get out of it. Life was certainly confusing.

He did not turn back. In a lonely spot he picked out a pine tree to address, and was no longer petrified by the sound of his voice. He talked with conviction. The Indian boy had become so real to him that he actually *wanted* to tell somebody, a captive audience even, about this redskin. *His* examination was worse than the College Boards', for if the boy failed to pass, he was classed with the squaws. *He* would have rescued the dog without hesitating to think.

It was too cold to give an encore. Savey walked back full of self-confidence and joy. He'd beat any impromptu speaker in the school, or any prepared one either. He was so confident and cold, that he decided to test his courage by stopping in at

Alcibiades' for some hot chocolate, out of bounds though it was.

The bar was noisy with Village youths. Some had been in a fight. They were being kidded by a couple of older fellows.

Savey listened. They were talking about the battered mongrel. Suddenly a name was mentioned, and he thrilled. He had to find out more. He got up nerve enough to walk over to these natural enemies and ask questions. They talked, they poured out the story. Savey was fascinated, deeply moved, and the light in his eyes eclipsed the fact that he was just another of "them rich boobs" up the Hill. Savey's whole being blazed with their account. He had money enough to buy cokes for the crowd. It was late and dark before he left. No time to eat, only time to dress. But he had been visited by an admiration so mighty that it drove the scaredness right out of his head.

*   *   *   *   *

The first sight of the auditorium brought it back. The aisles were lined with chairs, for the electrocution of innocent boys was always a popular spectacle. Chairs with people on them filled the platform. These spectators would be so near to the speakers that they could watch the victims tremble. It wasn't fair.

By tradition, the judges wore hard-boiled shirts. "To match their job" interpreted Hobey, who sat beside Savey in the front row. "Look at Harty. I bet he wouldn't hand Demosthenes 50% on his performance. Seen Vance yet, Save? He's back. He was looking for you." Savey had forgotten that

Vance was to be back in time to hear him. His nervousness doubled.

Harty explained the purpose and rules of the Contest for the visitors, then produced the first Isaac Ironwood's old top hat, and announced that the six speakers who were inaugurating their race for the White House would draw for places. To Savey's surprise, Steve Livey turned out to be one of the contestants. He drew first. The calling of Lily Waters' name was a far greater surprise, in spite of his successful Bible reading. He drew fifth place, Savey last.

Steve led off with an amusing account of life on a dude ranch from the cowboys' point of view. He rambled on colorfully and got laughs so continually that he became an obvious contender for the prize. Savey tested him by the written conditions—his clarity was complete, his steadiness of delivery perfect, he was naturally persuasive, but he could hardly be called forceful.

The next three speakers also declined to go impromptu. One drowned in self-consciousness, another forgot his lines too often, the third fizzled out. Savey breathed more easily. If Lily would kindly fold, he was in. Harty called "William Waters" and Savey noted, rather gladly, that the boy was paper-white as he stood behind the footlights. "Prepared or impromptu?" Harty asked.

"Impromptu, please, " came the strained voice. The audience clapped. The judges conferred. They must pick a subject which was fair to the speaker, yet one he could not easily tie in with preparation. A hush settled on the expectant crowd.

Harty straightened up and said, "The title of William Waters' speech is 'The Turning Point.' Proceed, Bill."

Savey sat tense with a divided mind. He sympathized with Lily and hoped he would not be too embarrassing a flop. Yet he earnestly wanted Lily to fail of the prize. Hobey whispered in Savey's ear, "A good thing Lily can't see her shadow, or she'd bolt the stage." Savey's whole attention was on the lanky, nice-looking youth who was quietly looking the house over.

Then he began in a voice that was even and easily heard. "This speech is true, as well as impromtu. But I use fictitious names. Anyone who tries to identify these persons will be sued for libel. Anyone who succeeds in identifying them will be carried from the room on a stretcher. Anyone who thinks he recognizes himself in them will be handed over to the police."

So unexpected and comical a warning coming from this particular boy convulsed the audience, and the ice was broken by enthusiastic applause. Savey stared in startled apprehension. This was serious. Hobey leaned close to him. "Listen to her! Do you suppose she filled up on firewater?"

Lily was saying, "It is noon of the day the new boys arrive. A skinny kid of fourteen enters by the wrong door and is taken in hand by the wrong crowd. The scared kid says, 'Will you please tell me which is boys' end?' 'Say *sir* when you address your betters,' commands Bunt Williams. 'What's your name?' 'Will Waters' the new kid says. 'From now on, fellows,' says Bunt, 'this shrinking flower is named Lily of the Valley. Lily for short. Now, Waters, what's your name?' 'Lily for short,' says the confused kid. 'Don't try to get fresh,' Bunt orders. 'It's Lily, and when you pass any of us in the hall, you hang your head in the way a drooping flowerlet should. Get me?' 'I'd like to,' the kid murmurs. 'Say SIR, SIR, *SIR*.' 'Sir, sir, *sir,*' the kid echoes.

"Fortunately for him, Hank Bennett came up then and Bunt says, 'Hank, this kid's shy. Ask him his name.' 'Well, what is it?' Hank asks impatiently. 'Speak when you're spoken to.' 'It's Lily, sir,' the kid says. Hank bellows out, 'Not good enough. Look down, look down, darn you, like a lily should.' *'And hang your asinine head,'* Bunt adds. 'This way.' He shows the kid how a modest flower should wilt at the neck. 'Now make like a lily,' he demands. The kid wilts and Hank says, 'He knows what's expected of him. Bunt, tell the rest of the gang to notify me if he freshens up. You may go now, Lily.'

" 'Will you tell me which way is boys' end?' 'SIR!' Shouts Hank. 'Don't forget that *sir*. There's a lake handy.' 'Sir, sir,' Waters repeats and is allowed to proceed in the direction offered—to the girls' end."

The audience laughed and Lily went on, "Young Waters had a lot to learn. He took the kidding, but didn't play the game. He took it too hard, and rebelliously side-stepped the right answers. When a dog chases a cat, the cat is supposed to show its claws and spit, and the dog respects it enough to let it go its way. But Lily gave no satisfaction, and his reformers called him yellow. He found himself looked down on and left coldly alone.

"One day Bunt met Lily in the woods. He felt sorry for the stray and said, 'Hello, Lily. Why don't you turn human again and hang around with the fellows?' 'Is that your definition of being human?' Lily snapped. 'That's a good crack, Bill'—and this was the first time in months that anyone but

the faculty had called the kid that, 'but it doesn't get you anywhere. Did it ever penetrate your educated nut that all the boys mightn't be wrong and only you right?' 'What's that to you?' Lily asked coldly for the months of what he thought was enmity had made him hard. 'Nothing at all,' Bunt retorted, 'except this: you came here to get educated, and you haven't wised up to the fact that part of an education is learning how to get along with people, how to make a place for yourself in the crowd.' Then Bunt went on and Lily Waters cried. He saw too late that he had not recognized a friend and had pushed him off. And there, in the woods, was the turning point in Will Waters' education. . . . I thank you all."

Utter silence for a few seconds, and then such applause as had not been heard in the Ironwood auditorium, the ovation to young Waters. It went on for minutes, and they were important minutes for Savey Miller. Lily's speech was a winner. No set speech could beat that quiet avowal of the shy boy who had made of himself a miracle of control, of rising to the occasion. Only an impromptu that was *better* had a chance, yet Savey had to win. He *had* to, or all his work on the Guide, all the help he had hoped to offer Vance, would go for nothing. Then the forgotten scene in the Village brought him a thought, an idea, a thunderbolt of inspiration, that raised the fur on his back.

"It was Vance," Hobey was saying to him. "Bunt Williams is Vance. Gosh, I'm glad he got back to hear that. There's your name, Save. Good luck, boy! This is *some* night." Savey saw that Hobey's eyes had been wet. Well, you never knew about a guy. Never.

152

Savey walked towards the judges, thinking "They'll give it to Lily or be lynched, so I don't have to think about that." This relinquishing of strain bolstered him up. He felt almost cool as he replied with that impossible word, "Impromptu," to Harty's question. A solitary hand clapping drew his attention; it was Vance. The audience joined in while the judges were conferring.

Harty rose and said, "The judges are quite proud of their success with the last title. We've now hit on another of equal promise. Savery Miller will speak on 'One Day in the Education of Savey Miller.'"

Savey pushed aside the feeling that he was getting infantile paralysis and said, "What I learn here in one day would require an equally long period of nonstop narration. I hope you've brought snacks, for today has been a succession of lessons. The judges have played into my hand by giving me this subject, and Bill Waters has assisted."

Savey then launched into a humorous account of his unwillingness to face an audience impromptu. He said that his hearers were going to miss a fascinating talk entitled "The Conditions of Self-Respect" which described the initiation of an Indian boy named Many Geese into manhood. He wished he could give that speech still, as it showed how lenient Ironwood's initiation was.

Another subject, he declared, was more pressing. He told of going out into the woods to rehearse the story of Many Geese before a pine tree, and of passing the Village boys tormenting the dog. He confessed, quite frankly, why he had not interfered. He also confessed to breaking the rule about entering Alcibiades' joint to thaw out on hot chocolate. A titter interrupted Savey here, and he saw that Master Harty was writing something down with an exaggerated frown.

Savey next explained why the Village toughs were so excited. A boy had interrupted their sport of shying missiles at the wounded dog, had told them to stop, had fought them all, and in his fury had bloodied noses, and knocked out the biggest of the gang. Then he had walked off with the dog.

Savey had thrilled over the way these toughs had swung over to the boy's side, praising his brainy way of making blows tell, and his guts in taking them all on. They recognized a man when they saw a real one.

"Since no one has threatened to carry me out on a stretcher for identifying the rescuer of that dog, I will risk it. I suggest that Vance Draper get up and lead the school in three salvos for—Lily Waters."

The thunderation that was unloosed by Savey's surprise beat the applause for Lily's speech. When Master Harty had let it run long enough, he stilled the crowd and said to Savey. "I see you still standing. Don't tell me there is more to come."

A laugh swept the room and Savey said, "Just one word more, the point. The point to my prepared talk was that the adult Indians who were initiating the boy by a severe and prolonged ordeal considered him manly until he proved otherwise. The law in this country works on the same basis. A suspect is held guiltless until he is found guilty.

"But the Ironwood system of initiation assumes that every new boy is a fresh nuisance until he can prove, against considerable odds, that he isn't. This system is un-Indian and un-American. I hope that my class, the junior class, will reverse this system and give every newcomer a chance to show

154

what he's like before jumping on him. This day in my education, as you can see, has been enriched by Bill Waters' splendid speech and by the toughs' acceptance of his splendid action."

The crowd applauded again and the judges retired to the rear of the stage to choose the winner. They were having a difficult time deciding, when suddenly a man near the front of the hall rose and said, "Honorable judges, may I be heard?"

"That's Andy Bellman's father," Hobey whispered to Savey.

Harty rose. "This is unusual, Mr. Bellman. But it has been an unusual evening. You may be heard."

"Sirs, I wish to make a three-minute speech which shall be obviously impromptu. Have I your permission?"

"This is still more unusual, Mr. Bellman. However, when last seen you were in your right mind, and we grant you three minutes on the condition that you're not adding to our troubles by competing for the prize."

The highly sensitized audience laughed and Mr. Bellman said, "Friends, I am sure that you are as astonished as I am by the forensic talent developed by this school. As impromptu speeches count double, I'm not trying to anticipate the judges' decision that the prize goes either to Mr. Waters or Mr. Miller. Thank heaven I'm not a judge. Off the record, I think it impossible to say which speech outdid the other in clarity, forcefulness, steadiness of delivery, and the ability to move us all. We have been deeply moved. I wish to offer a sum of money exactly equivalent to the prize to recompense the orator which you are forced by the rules to eliminate."

If Mr. Bellman had had more to say, he would not have been heard. Finally when Harty silenced the crowd, he said,

"Ladies and gentlemen, Ironwood School has never been known to refuse an offer of money honestly come by. As Mr. Bellman's income derives from the manufacture of an excellent brand of babyfood, it is appropriate that some of it should return to his customers in their more mature years. Consequently we are happy to accept his generous solution to our difficulties.

"The difficulties are obvious. The judges honor Bill Waters for the courageous revelation of his growth. The judges honor Savey Miller for his equally courageous revelation of his education. But one of the contestants has applied his idea to a larger situation that may influence the philosophy of the boys' end here. For that reason we announce him winner of the Contest by a hair. We are thankful indeed to Mr. Bellman for eradicating the loss that Bill might have had to sustain. If the gentleman does not happen to have his checkbook at hand, I can offer him a blank for the purpose."

More laughter, more applause which turned into tumult as Bill and Savey were called up to receive their rewards. Then order vanished in the rush of boys to surround the winner. With small reference to their best clothes, Savey and Lily were borne out of the auditorium on the stout shoulders of Ironwood's leading athletes.

*   *   *   *   *

Savey completed the one errand he had to do before climbing into bed. He was glad to accomplish it before Vance extricated himself from his cronies and came to his room. Savey had missed Vance much less the second week and now almost wished that he need not be bothered by Vance's press-

156

ing affairs. Such fickleness scared him. Could he continue to leave people he had cared for so easily as he had switched from Lola, said good-by at home, or even left his old, shy, studious, self-doubting self? Was this what growth did to you?

He lay there in a relaxed joy. How the dreadful burden of his daring to speak had turned into gold and given him the charge of his life! Imagine him, Savey Miller, carried on their shoulders, on *Sid's* shoulders! How his family would rejoice—and want to know what he'd do with the money. Even to his father $500 was a lot of money. Savey turned a little uncomfortable. He could not tell them about the book, or they'd expect to see it and—well, he was a man now. He'd show them the book, give them an autographed copy. What was it but life? After all, his father had been interested enough in girls to propose to his mother. But to sink his money in that! But it wouldn't be sunk. If other schools bought . . .

The door slammed open and Vance avalanched in. "Good gosh! You in *bed*? You ought to be celebrating. Come, let's crum off to Alcibiades and you can buy me a dinner. I've got to see the guy."

Savey's heart soured. Vance hadn't changed a bit. But *he* had. From now on he was going to respect the Ironwood rules. He was a public character now, respected by the finest man in Bucks County, Master Harty. But how to convince Vance that he had changed?

"I told you you had the goods, didn't I, didn't I?" Vance asked excitedly. "Boy, what a couple of politicians you and Lil are! He says how much this penitentiary has done for him, knowing it'd make the judges choke up. Then you go out for

157

kissing the brats as they arrive, and that's an even better bid for the money in this Quaker nursery."

Savey held in his disgust at Vance's interpretation of his and Lily's motives. "Weren't you proud when Lily made you the turning point?"

Vance hee-hawed. "I'm glad he acknowledged my services. I charge for them, and now he's rich."

"Did you earn the money to pay your debt, Vance?"

"Don't ask embarrassing questions. I worked but Dad pocketed the money for my bus fare. He called it discipline, not theft. Trust parents to put it over on you. By the way, Ordley asked me the same question. I told him I'd give him the whole fifty tomorrow. I suppose you haven't cashed that check yet?"

This was the moment Savey had dreaded, but he was a man now, he reminded himself. "I've a special use for that money, Vance."

If Savey had drawn a knife or broken his jaw with brass knuckles, Vance could not have been more surprised—or angrier. "But you can't do that! You can't hold out on me, Save! Who got you into the Contest? I only want fif—that is seventy-five bucks. You owe me that much."

"I'm sorry, Vance, but it's impossible."

Vance dropped his conciliatory air. "You've got to, pal. Ordley means business. You want to see me shipped home for keeps?"

Savey hesitated. "Ordley's in no position to get you fired."

"Stop backing out of your promises and come across."

"I never promised you a cent, Vance." Savey was almost

as angry as he was unhappy. "Anyway, the check's already in the mail."

Vance swore. "Of all the ungrateful, double-crossing flat tires! Who's been looking after you? Who snapped you out of your super-liliness and made you show what you've got?"

"If you have the sense you think you have," Savey said in a strange voice, "you won't make me mad. I thank you for a lot, Vance, and you'll benefit from what I've done. But you'll have to wait until after vacation. Now I'm tired and want to sleep."

Vance was speechless. The worm had turned, yeah, had turned into a snake, and bit him, *him*. This treason had to be considered, and in secret.

12 -

How to Woo an Iceberg

The spring term at Ironwood healed the wounds of winter. The seniors grew nostalgic, with the end in sight, and were allowed to study out of doors. The athletes had a choice of swimming, baseball, track, or tennis. The lake once more lapped happily at canoes. The girls made cakes and sent them to their dates at boys' end under armed guard. Funny Maxton relaxed. And for Savey Miller it brought nearer the publication date of his book.

He had made inspired arrangements for its distribution. The printer was to seek out Neil MacQuarrie and Scupper Riley in private and offer them a sturdy commission for peddling the book. These sophomores had seen proof sheets of an inciting chapter and were eager. They had stopped trying to guess the author and computed profits on any spare pieces of paper they saw lying around.

At last the day, or rather the evening! It was warm for so early in May, and Vance had taken his disciples outdoors to loll on the new grass behind the Meeting House. Hobey Tyler was airing a grievance. He admitted to a superior piece of folly at having forsaken the pliant Diane Ebbitts for beautiful Alicia Clements, but who could have guessed she was such a stick!

They listened to him gripe until bored and Vance said, "That shows how much you really know about girls. You still think they're sizzling Susies or cold numbers, like little Iceberg."

"Yeah? Well, scratch an iceberg and what do you get?" Hobey asked.

"*You* get scratched," Vance shot back, and the rest hooted.

Savey joined the five because he wanted to see what happened when Neil and Scupper reached them. He had gained in confidence, and they were friendly now with the new possessor of $500, but not only because they considered him well-heeled.

"Sit down, Save," Bud Tracy invited genially. "We're having an experience meeting. Found out anything new about the ladies?"

"I doubt if I could tell you much," Savey replied in the manner expected.

"You're an ex-iceberger," Hobey put in. "Why does Lola want to chill all comers by droves?"

"Don't ask me," Savey said. "All I know about women I learned from you."

"That's not enough, I'd say," Vance commented, and the others roared. Hobey's comeback was interrupted by the two sophomore salesmen carrying a basket nearly filled with pink-covered paper-backs whose gilt letters said:

A GUIDE TO GIRLS
or
WE TELL YOU HOW
by
Doc Wiley
$1

Neil distributed copies for inspection, and at once exclamations incredulous, humorous, and provocative, tickled Savey's very marrow. Tracy, who didn't have to watch the dimes, bought a copy for himself and one for Hobey, so that he could have the pleasure of saying, "Take it and learn, Hobe. It's worth a buck to shut you up."

Savey bought a copy and Vance at once took the book from his hands and started to peer at it condescendingly. Then he sat up and read in earnest. Then he pulled out a dollar and sait to Neil, "Who's Doc Wiley?"

"We weren't told. The printer just asked Scup and me to sell it."

Hobey let out a laugh. "Here's one for you, Vance. *How To Snare An Heiress.* The Doc knows his onions."

"Boy, O boy! This is love in ten easy lessons, or I can't read!" Tracy said.

Savey bit his tongue. There was a title he'd missed. "I bet you're not having any trouble unloading," Vance said to Neil.

"No, everybody's shelling out. Ginny's selling it at girls' end and they're sitting around screaming it out to each other."

"What's Teacher Minnie say to that?" Tracy asked.

"Need you ask?" Hobey retorted. "She'll get it confiscated."

162

"But I've got to know who wrote it," Vance said. "This is hot stuff. How many boarding schools are there? I'd like to be the guy's sales manager."

"I suspect he's an Ironwoodian," Bellman said. "Why get the Village printer if he came from a larger place?"

Savey felt a cold cloud pass over his satisfaction.

"He must be a grad, then," Vance observed. "Nobody we know is this good, not even Save here."

The bell rescued Savey before his face flushed, but that evening after lights out Vance said to his roommate, "I begin to smell a rat, Save. You told me to wait for something. Remember? Could this be it?"

"Yes, Vance," Savey said. "I wrote it—with your help. It's dedicated to you."

"Me?" Vance turned to the first page and read "To One Who Helped." My first dedication—and last. My hat's off to you, Save. It's really something."

"I'm going to give you fifty bucks as soon as the money comes in," Savey went on. "Promise you won't tell anyone?"

"I promise. I'll do more than that. I'll give you the time of your life tomorrow night. And will that fifty come in handy!"

*　　*　　*　　*　　*

Wonders kept coming, even in so outwardly simple a place as Ironwood School, Savey thought. Most of the wonders depended, though, on breaking rules. Here he was crumming in the tunnel, when he should be studying in his room. Still more remarkable, he was listening to Master Harty, far off in the Green Room, and being admitted into the faculty's secret discussions was more miraculous than anything he had experienced.

It was also more dangerous. Vance had enticed him into the trap without saying anything more than, "Mind coming with me, Save? I think you're being talked about." He had followed like the lamb he fancied he had outgrown. He should have refused to crum, and certainly have refused to enter the tunnel. Now he had this outrageous crime on his conscience. Eavesdropping was low. Eavesdropping on a faculty meeting was equal to a one-way ticket home. And Vance knew it! He had played into Vance's hand, like a simpleton.

Since he was here, Savey told himself, he might as well listen, but never again was he going to break a rule. Master Harty was saying, "I have here a remarkable booklet whose authorship, like the plays of Shakespeare, is in doubt. Is there anyone present who hasn't seen a copy?"

"How could there be?" Teacher Minnie retorted sharply. "The school is flooded with the unspeakable thing. There will be no homework done for days. I propose that the copies be gathered and held until school closes."

"Isn't that a little too reminiscent of the Nazis?" Blaik McClintock asked.

"Then you favor this vulgarity to be circulated in a school whose duty is to watch over its wards?"

"Aren't you overstating the matter?" Blaik asked smoothly.

Master Harty's voice broke in. "I've read this little gem twice. There is nothing vulgar in it. The author has kept one eye on nature, the other on the book of etiquette, and then steered a careful passage between."

"I don't agree with you," Minnie said.

"Take my copy and read us a passage you view with disfavor."

"I decline to waste our valuable time on the obvious."

Suddenly Coach Kress gave an irrepressible snort. "What is it you find so funny, George?" Harty asked and his tone gave Savey the impression that he was making fun of Teacher Minnie.

"This chap, this Doc Wiley," stuttered the coach, "he sure knows his ankles—excuse me, I mean angles. Listen to this:

> "We come now to the difficult assignment of dating a girl with more money than you have. It is the sport of kings on a schoolboy's allowance. Go back to our fundamental axiom, that romance is desired by all, by the rich as well as the poor.
>
> "It is not invariably true that rich girls have no brains. A few may have, but you must assume that *all* have, and your prospect in particular. This will delight and probably surprise her, and you score one.
>
> "The grand difficulty in snaring an heiress is her fixed idea that you have her money in view. You can't help having it, for she looks it and talks it and breathes money down your back, should you get that close. Therefore the masterstroke lies in ignoring it. Pretend to yourself, night and day, that she is poor. Never, *never* accept a penny of it in the all too easy ways. Never go Dutch, as you may with a poor girl. This will entrance her and her parents alike. Score two."

"That will have to do," Harty broke in. "The author is giving a simple course in psychology. I'm not sure that we shouldn't have him on the staff."

"There are passages I do not understand," Cecil Maxton broke in. "When he advises on how to woo an iceberg . . ."

Savey was gratified by the laughter from the assembly. Teacher Minnie interrupted them with, "Isaac Ironwood cannot return too soon, in my opinion. This spirit of levity on serious matters is undermining the school. The chapter that Cecil Maxton refers to is obnoxious in the last degree."

Master Harty said to the dean of boys, "Since you know our end of the school better than Minnie, Henry, do you consider the passage subversive to our morals?"

"Read it," Vanner said. "I haven't had time."

Savey now heard his carefully selected words given a just rendering by the voice of command:

"Some girls are cool by nature and some are made so by their relatives. But the fellow who cannot bring a chilly number back to normal must class himself with the flat tire, the frosted cabbage, or the defunct bulb. The iceberg is not to be confused with the timid or cautious skirt. (See Chapter 8, Conquest of the Prude). The prude is afraid of others, the iceberg is afraid of herself. For the former we advised the oblique approach—sympathy laced with instruction. But the iceberg, floating along in her arctic surroundings, needs only understanding company more or less continuously applied. The suitor must be patient, persistent, and practical. One has only to study elementary geography to learn that icebergs melt in warmer waters."

Savey blushed at having exposed Lola Wilson to the laughter that followed Harty's reading. He had felt sure that she had never heard her nickname; and after her opening the window to scatter his pages, he was so angry that he did not care. But now, in his hour of triumph, he felt contrite.

"Will someone in the English Department tell us who is able to write like that?" Harty asked. "Andrew, whom do you suspect?"

Andrew Cliff considered. "I'm at a loss to say, Wilfred. It would be mature for my best writer."

"Cecil, do you harbor such a prodigy in your classes?"

"None who can sustain a style like that, unless it is Savery."

"I shouldn't dream of accusing him!" Teacher Minnie interrupted indignantly. Savey looked at Vance in the lantern light and grinned back, though rather frozenly.

"I'm not accusing him," Funny Maxton retorted.

"I doubt that Savey is equipped to write 77 pages on the opposite sex," Henry Vanner said.

Kress agreed. "True, though Savey's coming along since our friend here released him to Cornelia, but . . ." the rest was lost in the laughter from the others at his jest at Lola's expense.

"I know who wrote the book!" Lola declared to the electrification of all.

Cries of "Do tell!" "A girl or a boy?" "Come across."

"What do you propose to do to the author?" Lola asked Harty.

"I might ask him to contribute part of his profits to the Scholarship Fund," Harty replied, amid general laughter. "We want more boys of his caliber, if it is a boy. Will you impart the name?"

Savey shuddered and failed to hear what Lola said.

Harty pounded on the desk. "I didn't hear. Please repeat."

"I said that I obtained the knowledge unfairly, and do not feel free to violate his anonymity—*though I'd like to*," she finished with more than a trace of wrath.

"So it is Savey," Kress said, to more laughs.

"It *isn't* Savey!" Minnie Winters cried. "I won't have our one really good boy falsely accused. I deplore nothing more than the tendency to smirch the character of others by gossip."

"It depends on the point of view," Harty responded. "Why bar normal life from a boarding school? If we've been educating our students as wisely and thoroughly as they deserve, this analysis of various attitudes can harm nobody. These pages are really healthy satire. Let me read the conclusion:

> "The point of all this is something that never gets mentioned in bull sessions and yet is the thing that counts most: it's discovery. Everybody is looking for a friend—or should be. The wise boy chooses the girl he thoroughly respects, and she helps him maintain his self-respect. Such friendship is just about the best thing one can have while growing up. I hope that some girl who reads this will write 'A Guide To Boys.' We need to learn a lot. Amen."

168

Savey felt a little choked at the praise Harty was giving him when he was doing something unworthy. He was ashamed of listening in, yet he wouldn't have missed this knowledge so gained for anything. Life was certainly complicated. One thing, though: no more crumming, no more hiding his views of right-doing from Vance out of a cowardly reluctance. He decided to make good on his vow at once. He tapped Vance and said with his lips, "I'm going."

Vance took off his headphone. "Why the rush?"

"I don't think it's decent, listening in like this."

"Don't be a Minnie! Didn't you just find out that Little Iceberg's semi-human—not giving you away? I call that worth smooching in for."

Savey started off, lest he yield to the impelling temptation to hear more about himself. He had a way of telling what was wrong by imagining how he'd feel if found out. He couldn't endure having Harty summon him to the Office and say, "I can't believe it of you, Savey." No punishment Harty could give, short of sending him home, could be as bad as that look. Savey hurried, banging his shin in the dusty dark.

*　*　*　*　*

"You're making that up!" Ginny Erdwin exclaimed to Diane Ebbits. "How could they rig up wires and all that with hundreds of people around? You're just sore, Di, because Hobey slinks off with Alicia. I warned you. Hobe's short for Hobo. He's a tramp under that smile. How did you get down there?"

"The tunnel belonged in old Fort Ironwood, you know. I read about it in an old *Blue and Gold*. I told Bagley I was doing a piece for the *Blue and Gold*."

"Hate certainly makes you industrious," Ginny observed.

"I don't hate him. I'm trying to." Diane's voice went limp. "I'd take him back in a minute."

"That's why he hunted up the new party," Ginny said scornfully. "The boys like a little resistance. Won't you ever learn?"

"Your Vance is in it too. There were two headphones, and of course Hobey can't do anything without Vance. Another thing: Hobe was trying to build himself up with Alicia and let drop that he and Vance had been real devils the night before Christmas vacation ended. They slept at Alcibiades' joint."

Ginny stiffened. "So that's it! The missing clue. So they came here when there weren't hundreds of people at work. I get it."

"And *I* have their headphones. I sneaked them out under my skirt. That'll start them thinking."

"You're a genius!" Ginny exclaimed. "We could pry them right out of this school, if they get too fresh. So you'd take Hobey back, would you?"

"I'm not sure," Diane wavered.

"I'll scare him so he'll crawl back, if you like."

"I don't think I'd like. I really went for that boy, Gin."

Ginny gave a shrill unladylike laugh. "If you've never kept a secret, you're beginning now, honey. Just put those big eyes away and pretend nothing. Don't do any pieces about tunnels for the *B & G,* either. This is going to be very, *very* good."

*   *   *   *   *

170

Savey was backed against the window sill of his room. Hobey had clutched his wrist, and Vance, dark with anger, stood in front of him. Savey hoped that they didn't see how sick with alarm he was. They were going to beat him up, because they were frightened, too, and didn't believe him. But he said it again, "I don't know one thing about the headphones. I didn't take them."

"You lie," Hobey cried and his handsome face was pallid with angry dismay. "If anybody else had played this trick on us, it would've been all over the place in ten minutes. The mike's gone, too."

"I don't even know where it was," Savey said despairingly.

"It's too late to act the innocent," Vance's deeper voice said. "You knew where it was. Just confess, and we won't take you apart."

"I told nobody. I know nothing about it. Have I ever lied to you?"

"I'll twist your arm off if you make me any madder," Hobey said in a fury of bad conscience. "If Bags had found anything, he'd have told Harty and we'd be on the carpet before now. If any boy had stumbled on them, he'd have listened in and yelled about it. Nobody knew but you. You told Vance you wanted none of it. Vance told me you'd gone Minnie on us and might spill the news on account of your filthy white conscience. Now come across." Hobey tightened his hold on Savey's wrist and started to twist.

"Ouch. Stop that!" Savey writhed to counteract the pressure.

"Come across, I say."

A cry of sudden pain burst from Savey's lips. "Shut up, and spill it quick." Hobey's face was hard and white.

"Watch out, don't break his arm," Vance cautioned.

The door opened as Savey sank to his knees to ease the torture. "Stop that!" Colt demanded as he strode into the room.

"Get out. You're not wanted." Vance pushed Colt against the bunk. Colt knocked him away and clouted Hobey's chin so sturdily that he let go of his victim. Savey collapsed on the floor, holding his arm.

"Butt out of this," Vance demanded in turn and lunged at Colt. Hobey attacked from the other side, and a wild melee ensued. The noise brought spectators, and among them Henry Vanner. He and Sid Dalton managed to separate the fighters. Vance's nose was gushing blood. Hobey's right eye had swollen. Colt licked bleeding lips.

"What now?" the dean of boys flung at Vance between breaths.

"A slight difference of opinion," Vance retorted. The last thing he wanted was to explain.

"Hobey, why are you fighting?" asked the irate master.

"I don't know, sir. It was a mistake."

Henry Vanner knew that he must not take this cool insolence or lose the last shreds of respect. He tried Colt. "Will you tell me what you're doing in this room?"

"I heard Savey cry out, looked in, found Hobey twisting his arm and stopped it."

Vanner turned to the victim. "Savey, you must know why your arm was being twisted."

Vance and Hobey literally stopped breathing. Savey

172

controlled his features enough to reply, "It was a mistake, sir, as Hobey told you. I don't want to say anything more."

Vance jumped in with, "If Hobey and I promise to consider it settled, will you call it off too, sir?"

Henry Vanner was only too glad to avoid digging farther and was about to assent when Colt said, "You can't drop it like this, sir. Savey was being seriously hurt. He'll be hurt again—when nobody's around."

"What do you think we are, a pack of wolves?" Vance's hatred of Colt shone in his eyes. "Hobe and I were in the wrong. We know that now. I guarantee that Savey will not be molested. Let them kick us out of this dump if we go back on our word. Isn't that right, Hobe?"

"I agree."

"Is that satisfactory to you, Colt?" Master Henry asked.

"If Savey is satisfied." He looked at the pale boy.

Savey nodded, too near tears to speak. Vance, who had stood aside and doubted him, had hurt him worse than Hobey's ferocity. He had lost a friend forever—a strange sort of friend whom he had to differ with but somehow loved.

"Now go to the Infirmary and get fixed up," Vanner said to the wounded boys.

Colt waited until Vance and Hobey had gone and said, "Do you want to change roommates, Savey? I can't guess what's the matter, but I don't want you living under a threat."

This sympathy was the bit too much. Savey conquered a sob but could only say, "Thanks, Colt. I can't tell you about it. Vance'll stick by his word. I guess I'll go outdoors now."

13 –
Spring, Beautiful Spring!

Coach Kress was feeling good. The 7 to 5 victory over George School with Ian MacQuarrie pitching the whole way gave him hope. Vance had been errorless at first base, Dalton as dependable as ever at center field, and Hobey as good a third baseman as he'd ever had. Westtown had barely licked George School by a 3 to 2. This was the year to achieve the big dream—a season of no defeats. He'd never have it so good again, for Ian and half the team would graduate in three weeks.

Hobey was feeling good. He had settled down. Boys' end was openly talking of him as the coming Student Body President. Oh, that car! He wanted it more than anything else, unless it was Diane. He longed to have her back. He was tired of Alicia's treacle, "Yes, honey; I know, honey." Honey, honey, honey, bah! But Diane was acting strangely, for her. He hadn't expected her to be pleased at being given the air.

But everybody made mistakes, yet she continued to snoot him —even after his flawless game against George School. Ginny was giving Vance a working-over, too. It must be the spring that was making them feel high. Vance was good and sore. That of course was very funny. The great, all-conquering wise guy Vance!

Colt was not feeling good. He had been weak to give in to Master Harty about the Student Body Presidency—and then Council—and now baseball, with homework piling up. How come he was doing everything he had agreed with himself not to do? And now Ian MacQuarrie was due in a minute to explain to him the intricacies of the S.B.P. campaign. Ian was to be his manager, if Colt was nominated.

Ian opened the door. Colt felt the impact of the boy's personality before he spoke. Ian had grown in depth. Colt had never admired him more than in the game with George School, for Ian had called up reserve after reserve to go the distance, had not wasted a motion, nor an emotion, either. Colt said to himself that to work with Ian in the coming tussle lessened the sting of sacrificed work and its uselessness, for it was clear that he wouldn't be nominated.

"You'll be nominated," Ian grinned openly. "The boys'll pick Hobey, Brick Evans, and perhaps Tracy. But Council nominates the other two, and I've sounded the members out. We're going to nominate you and Bellman. That's this coming Monday. Each boy will be given a ballot on which he writes down the names of two boys he'd like to see lead boys' end next year. The girls are doing the same thing at girls' end.

"Then on Wednesday each candidate gives a speech to

the Boys' Assembly. That's the big moment. It's your bid for office. Your personality's on inspection, your mental calibre, your showmanship."

"But what's the speech on?"

"That's up to you. Sometimes the candidate goes all out for reforms, possible and impossible, usually about dating. He promises more dating time, less supervision. It's an open bid for election, and it fools some. But the fellows really try to pick the best guy, even if Ordley did get it."

"Give me a steer," Colt requested.

"Use your experience in Council to suggest your line. You can outline a better attitude towards punishments, or talk about lessening the tightness of cliques, or a finer school spirit. What you're saying is 'if you fellows vote for me, I'll help make Ironwood a finer, or happier, or freer place.' "

"Gosh!" Colt said thoughtfully—more work ahead.

"On Thursday, the candidates sit on the platform again and the boys throw questions at them. They're making up their minds. Some of the questions are mighty searching, too. And after them, Council hands its own questions to the candidates. No candidate may get help answering these questions. The answers are read on Friday night to the Boys' Assembly. Friday's a big night, for there's a 'Beat Westtown' pep rally."

"I'll say," Colt commented.

"Then on Saturday night, after the ball game, comes your crisis—the elimination elections. The three fellows who get the most votes go into the final week, Campaign Week. Vance will do his darndest to eliminate you."

"You can count my votes on your fingers and toes," Colt said.

"Go brainwash yourself!" Ian smiled. "I'm going to elect you with my secret weapon. Do you know Ellen Waring well?"

Colt grinned. "That's changing the subject."

"Not a bit. She's my kingmaker. She's going to be S.B.P. at girls' end. Twice is unusual but she's sure. Vance'll try to get the girls to influence their dates over here for Hobey. I'm your able manager, don't forget, and I'll get *Ellen* to influence the girls to influence their dates to vote for you. And Ellen's a lot more liked over there than Ginny and Diane. You'll see that you're one of the three chosen for the final showdown."

"Big politics!" Colt grinned, suddenly lifted and happy that he and Ellen would have this new bond.

"It's war with very little blood," Ian said.

Colt straightened up. "You win. Ellen wins. Harty wins. And *I'll* win—just to make it unanimous. I pledge you that, Ian."

The two friends looked at each other and Ian thought: *This is going to be something.*

*　　*　　*　　*　　*

"There is such a thing as growing up," Ginny said to Diane.

Di's black eyes glittered. "Oh, stop it! I hate him and that's that."

"Of course you do, darling," Ginny pursued relentlessly. "We all do, except those who don't know him and want to." It was dark in the room and Ginny was worn. This bickering had gone on for days.

"Alicia *crows* so!" Diane snapped back.

"As I remarked, sweetheart, there's such a thing as growing up. I know you could blow Hobey out of this school, simply by leaving the headphones in Harty's office with a little note—unsigned, of course. But it's a snake's way of getting back at your ex-date, and unfortunately it might also end Vance's stay at this school. Which is where I come in. I'd never forgive you, Di. What's more, Hobey'd never forgive you—and he's really only taking a vacation from you. And what's most important you'd never forgive yourself."

"I don't care. It serves him right."

"You'd like a hundred girls laughing at you?"

"You're crazy!" Diane's head came up in the dark. "Who'd know?"

"Do you think I'd sit by and let you can Vance? They'd know and look at you in disgust."

"I'm not convinced."

Ginny gave up, exhausted. "Let's not talk any more. I'm done in, Di. Go to sleep. We can both see better in the morning."

Dead as she was, Ginny was too scared to sleep. She must act. She'd learned from Vance to plan ahead and now she had a job to do that frightened her, but Di frightened her worse.

So, when she was sure that Diane was sound asleep, Ginny slipped from bed, lifted the flashlight noiselessly from the drawer, waited until the night watchman passed, stole down to Diane's locker, read the combination which she had long ago procured, opened the door, lifted the headphones and the mike into a long towel, and, shivering with fright and chill, went out into the ghastly night.

They sank quickly into the lake.

Ginny shook with terror as something swooped past her head. She ducked and ran, perilously, through the dewy grass, pursued she was certain by owls, bats, spiders, and the other horrors that an insane Nature had created to scare willful girls. She only reached the school alive by thinking of Vance, of his arm about her. His were hardly sheltering arms, but strong. It was a pity, it was irony of the cruelest sort, that she couldn't tell him what had become of the headphones. But it was not her policy to let Vance off easy. She was a strong-minded girl, Ginny was. And she had to look out for him.

14 -
The Pay-Off

Alcibiades took the phone. His head ached. You had to drink to hook a big customer. He thought the drive out from Jersey City would split his head, with the sun in his face. But the trip had been necessary and worth-while. No schoolboy was going to tell him what he should do. "Yes, yes," he said into the phone.

"This you, Al?"

"Yes."

He listened to the voice. "Seven o'clock'll fix it."

He forgot his headache and thought he hadn't heard right. Then he said, "Sure, sure. I can tip you off to the guy, Shank."

Alcibiades replaced the phone. He'd fix the big butt-in. For keeps. The head-throb knocked back into his consciousness, but this was worth it. Shank and Suds! All you had to do was know the right ones. They took care of things for you. He walked into the kitchen where his brother was cleaning up. "Want to see the ball game?"

Nestor looked up in surprise. "Sure, but I got work."

"I got work for you. Nice work you like."

Their looks met in understanding. "I heard the phone. That him?"

"Sure. I told you. He'll be here before seven, and a guy to help, name of Suds. He's just out of stir. Come in now and I show you what I fix you do."

*　*　*　*　*

The month of May had supplied a day worthy of the big game. The dry air basked in its own sunny stillness. Long yellow buses had brought almost two hundred Westonians. In the opposing grandstand sat three hundred Ironwoodians in massed tension. In front of them a row of blue backs indicated that Ironwood was at bat. Coach Kress hoped that he could keep his sanity for the remaining innings. This was doubtful.

He had been watching almost professional ball. For six taut innings the play had been tight, fast, clean—and scoreless. Something had to break soon. Never had he seen one of his pitchers complete a no-hit game, nor any other schoolboy, either. Ian MacQuarrie was as cool as Kress had seen him under a cold shower. Only this was a hot bath.

A concerted groan from the stands at his back indicated that Sid Dalton had struck out. Hobey had struck out ahead of Sid. Vance ahead of Hobey. The power plant had busted.

"All right, boys," Kress said as the blue backs rose. He daren't say anything more. You couldn't improve perfection by a syllable. The nine had made so accurate a piece of clockwork out there that half a syllable might mar the moving pendulum's beautiful regularity.

Colt, still sitting, felt a tightness across his chest, a petrified lump in his throat, an almost unendurable tension in his head. This was no game, it was a subtle torture that stretched each nerve a bit farther by the minute. He hoped for a break in Ironwood's favor soon. He prayed that Ian would last. The magnificence that Colt had always felt in the dark handsome boy on the mound was there revealed. This was his last game for Ironwood, his great day. Kress must have the same faith in Ian, for he had not yet signaled Colt to start warming up.

"Strike three."

The Ironwood stand applauded. Ian relaxed in the sunlight. It had been Vance's big day, too. He had speared a dangerous liner. He and Hobey, across there at third, had thwarted another threat between them. Colt, forgetting past irritations, looked at them and saw their self-forgetfulness, the concentration in their faces. This was a peak of living and each individual on the team out there in the sun felt it.

"Strike three."

One more to go. Colt took no credit in the skill of Ian's pitching, though he had helped perfect it. A pupil like Ian wasn't really a pupil, but another you.

Colt was watching when the Westtown batter connected. Ian's right hand shot up, in an instinctive *must,* regardless of glove. The ball found that hand in its way, and stopped. Ian dropped to the ground, but still clutching it. Two fingers had been broken.

Kress waved Colt to the pen. They seated Ian on the bench, for he refused to go in. Colt completed his warm up. Inning eight began. But the tail of the batting order could not accomplish what the giants, Dalton and Hobey and

Vance, had failed in attempting. Ironwood fanned and Colt walked to the mound. In a world suddenly bristling with dangers, one assurance stood him in good stead: he *could* pitch. He sank his practice throws in Steve Livey's mitt with a concentration that shut out the stands. It was good to have Steve, the unbrilliant, the utterly dependable, as the other part of him.

Colt got the signal. The ball left his hand. The bat's sound was sharp, solid—the crack of doom. Colt didn't have to look. The stands rose. Sid, racing back, was still short by yards. A homer. Westtown 1 . . . Ironwood 0.

Probably it was like this, Colt thought, when lightning struck you. He stood, helpless, dazed, numbed, an awful nausea fogging his whole being. The first he knew was Steve close in front, saying fiercely, "It's just one. Nobody on base. Just one. They'll think you're easy. Ride herd on them, fellow."

Silence again. Colt raised his arms; Steve pulled it straight, but the umpire said, "Ball one." The next pitch was a hook that broke across the pan. The third was a bit below the knees. "Ball two." Steve asked for a repeat but higher. The batter bopped it up and Steve had it easily. The next was the real Colt; the batter was about five minutes late on the swing.

The Ironwood stands applauded, little thinking that the game was practically over. In the ninth, Westtown weakened to the extent that Colt reached second on a clean hit to left field, and Vance almost knocked him home—but didn't, and the game was over. Westtown 1 . . . Ironwood 0—a tragedy that made the last act of Hamlet look like a love scene.

Kress was at his magnanimous finest in the lockerroom,

while the wolf of disappointment sharpened its fangs on his liver. "You never played better," he told the dejected dressers. "Nor did Westtown. Never in half a century have I seen anything to beat this day's play."

"They wheel you to the ball park in a baby-rig, Coach?" Steve asked, for Kress was fifty-one. It got the first small laugh.

"It was my fault," Kress said to Colt as the boys began to leave. "I should've had you warm up sooner. I was just mesmerized. You got to be yourself mighty soon."

"They counted on me, and I didn't make it for them," Colt said. "Ten tons of alibis won't change the score."

"They saw you pull out of it, too."

Colt changed the subject. "Is Ian waiting for the doctor?"

"Brick Evans' father's fixing him up. He's a big surgeon, you know. He'll be on hand for the eliminations tonight."

"Gosh! I forgot!" Colt's jaw sagged. "Ian's my manager. He's baby-nursed me through the week. There aren't any more speeches tonight, are there?"

"No, you just sit on the platform and look pretty. Master Ike always made a three-minute speech about the seriousness of choosing candidates. Probably Master Harty will. After two of you are eliminated, the three left begin campaigning, but mostly with posters. Ian's probably got yours made."

"I told him it was wasted effort. And now I've eliminated myself by that pitch."

Kress wanted to put his hand on his shoulder but something in Colt stopped this. Kress said, "A man never gives up till the count's in, son. And you're as much man as we've had here. There's not an ounce of yellow in you."

184

"Isn't reason permitted?" Colt asked. "Is straight think-ing forbidden? My father taught me to face facts."

"All right, face them. You're going to face a hundred and fifty boys, of all sorts, and they have x-ray eyes. Sure they let their feelings run off with their intelligence. They like Hobey because he's easy-going and snags the girls the way he pulls in a fly ball. But they know in their hearts that he's no one to sit in judgment on them. They want, in their hearts, someone they can trust, really trust down deep. Brick's a fine boy but he lacks experience. The candidates are all good for one thing or another. But you're a man, and all they need is to have their eyes opened a bit wider. Master Harty will probably do that."

"I thought it was sure death if the faculty rooted for you."

"That's right. Harty won't mention you. He won't even hint at a preference. He'll say what Master Ike says. But it will be said in a way that sinks in. Have you seen Ian's posters?"

Colt shook his head. "He didn't want me meddling."

"Quite right. You'd have tempered them down. It's no time for modesty." Kress chuckled. "He showed me a few. I'm not giving a confidence away, for you can't do anything about them now. They go up tonight, the minute the votes are counted."

"Break the news. I can take it." Colt almost smiled, for Kress had eased him back a little to his normal self-reliance.

"One of them states, in letters two feet high: BE ABLE TO TELL YOUR CHILDREN YOU VOTED FOR COLT."

Colt did smile. "He's sure looking ahead."

"Another says, BACK THE COLT IN THIS RACE AND CLEAN UP. That's good double-talk for they'll know he's referring to Ordley. Then there's a banner that will hang just outside the Assembly Room, TAKE A HOLT WITH COLT. That's also a reform cry. I like best the one that doesn't even mention you. STEVE ROPED A WINNER."

"They sound like Neil's work to me," Colt said.

Kress chuckled again. "OUR SCOT'S IN THE SLOT. Wonderful! Ian hasn't underrated the boys' intelligence. They like to be made to think—at times, anyway. STEVE ROPED A WINNER is as good a campaign ad as I remember, for Steve is a fellow to tie to. He caught a perfect game. A man is known by his friends. Now there's the bell. You'll have to skin out of those duds fast. I'll leave you alone."

Colt said, "Thanks, Coach. Not so much alone as I was."

* * * * *

"Let's go," Hobey said from the doorway of Vance's room. He was cunningly dressed to look careless and be his handsomest.

Vance glanced up from the poster he was finishing and approved. "I've got two letters to ink in. You go ahead. When you sit facing the mob don't think of them, and still less of yourself. Think of Alicia, or that car."

"Alicia forever!" Hobey waved an imaginary flag.

"Until after the voting, anyway," Vance smiled. "You certainly made it hard for me by changing horses in midstream. Diane's still out for your scalp, Ginny tells me. Ginny's handing out the raspberry too." Vance dipped brush in the ink. "Girls are worse than elephants when it comes to not

186

forgetting. Ginny's still trying to find out what we did the night we came back to rig up the hearing-aid. I think she knows about that, Hobe. She keeps dropping hints as big as coconuts."

"If she knew, they wouldn't be hints."

"She told me she wanted to know what the faculty were saying about smoking recently, and would I kindly over-hear?"

"She did?" Hobey was amused. "And you said?"

"I said that only a donkey had ears that long, and was she trying to call me one? I told her I valued frankness, and that sent her into hysterics."

"They'll do anything to get attention," Hobey remarked.

"She also said that Alcibiades' brother brought her some of the weed and had quite a chat. Ginny told him that it wasn't our fault that we quit buying cigs but Colt's. He gummed the works. Nestor said that Alcibiades knew that and would like to give Colt a good punch in the jaw. I told her to tell the Greek to do his punching soon."

"It would be a help."

"Not that you need worry." Vance reached for a paper on the bureau. "Nicky took a straw poll. There are 151 boys, so you need 76 to be elected. And you have 92, as of now. It's almost certain that tonight's vote will eliminate Colt, so you're S.B.P. sure. Sit there with that news on your face so everybody can read it."

"Gosh, that's swell news," Hobey said. "I'll even lend you the car."

"The least you can do is to get your family to buy two, one for me. There, how do you like this one?" Vance held up the completed poster. STAY SANE: VOTE FOR HOBEY. "I've been telling them what sanity means—more and better dating, hay rides, sleigh rides, a good dance band from Trenton, some really hot speakers for General Assembly, less faculty supervision at dances. You might suppose Minnie didn't trust us."

Hobey laughed. "When do we put up the posters?"

"Nicky's got a crew just waiting for the word. They'll be up twenty minutes after the vote's counted. Now step on it, Hobe. Be first on the old platform. I'll go wash up and be right down."

Ink takes time to remove from human flesh, and the corridors were strangely quiet by the time Vance was dressed. A little lateness did not matter. *He* wasn't sitting on the platform. He merely pulled the strings and Ironwood did his bidding. Hobey was in, if Nicky's straw vote was accurate. Colt would certainly be eliminated. Neither Tracy nor Brick Evans had quite what it took to swing a popular vote. More boys wanted fun than long faces. Ordley had overdone being easy. But he was a stinker anyhow. Hobey had class. He'd look well behind the wheel in his new car.

Vance admired himself in the mirror as he combed his hair. He wasn't taking anybody's dust from now on. As he stepped out into the corridor, he spotted two young men four or five doors away, looking at the numbers. Vance stared at these queer characters as if they'd strayed from another world. They had a sort of hyena look. The taller one wore pronounced sideburns, and a cigarette sagged from a hard mouth. Both wore the tight, smarty clothes never seen far from the tough end of small towns. Yet they had too bold an air to be thieves. "What do you want?" he called.

They started at the voice. "Colt Muir's room. A guy said 31."

Vance's dislike of these invaders mounted. "He's not there," he said shortly.

The head hyena pulled open the door without knocking. Vance's quick temper flared. It was one thing for him to buck Colt and shove him out of Hobey's way; but these strangers had a nerve to act as if they owned the dorm. "I told you he wasn't there." Vance went towards them to stop whatever they had in mind. "Colt's in the Assembly room downstairs."

"Not three minutes ago he wasn't," the shorter one said.

"What do you want?" Vance asked roughly. He smelled liquor on them and his suspicion of something serious grew.

They ignored his question and the short one said, "We better wait in his room, Shank."

"He won't be back for hours," Vance said. He had no notion of leaving these hard nuts unwatched. "I'll take you to him."

"I better go tell the boss," the short one said to Shank. "He don't like waiting."

"He'll wait," Shank said, then to Vance, "Okay."

Vance was in a hurry and led the way down the corridor to the stairs. As they neared the Lavatory at the head of the stairs, they heard steps on the tiled floor. Vance looked in and saw Colt, and stepped in to warn him of his tough visitors. The taller one caught sight of Colt and said to his partner, "Here he is, Suds," and added something under his breath that Vance couldn't hear. Vance saw Colt suddenly stop, as if he had come to an unexpected precipice, and he let the coat he was putting on drop to the floor. "Shank . . . Suds . . . you here?"

Shank said, "We got lonesome for you, Colt." The look in Shank's hardened young face was unmistakable now, a mixture of ferocity and gloating. Vance felt his throat tighten. These must be the Hi-Gunners that he, in an angry moment, had wanted to summon to get Colt out of his way.

Colt said to Vance, but without taking his eyes off Shank, "You'd better go down now. You'll be late."

Shank said to Vance, "Don't go. We like your company."

Vance's ordinarily quick mind was frozen. Could he help Colt by raising a warning better than by sticking with him? Then he glanced at the doorway and saw Suds standing in it with a revolver in his right hand. He was trapped.

"That's right," Shank's partner said. "Stick around."

"You're out of your territory," Colt said to Shank.

"Red Mahovey sent me to bring you in. You were dumb to get in the Greek's way, Colt."

Vance suddenly understood. Alcibiades had sent word to this Red Mahovey, who was in jail, of Colt's whereabouts, and Red had tipped off these killers. Vance felt sick, for he had, in his wrath, shown Alcibiades the news clipping of Colt's Hi-Gunner past.

"Put on your coat," Shank ordered Colt. "Now this is it, you two. We've got a car down at the foot of the fire escape. You're both coming quiet. You won't get hurt, unless you try something. If you get funny, it'll be just too bad. Have it your way," he added. "It don't matter to us."

190

"I'll come if you'll let my friend here alone." Colt offered. "He's done nothing to hurt you."

"How long'd he keep his puss shut?" Shank asked. "Be yourself."

"You could tie him. It'd give you an hour."

"Quit the jabber," Suds said nervously from the doorway.

Vance's wits were running around in his head like mice in an attic. What could he do? Without the guns, he and Colt had a chance, although Shank's two hundred pounds of bone and brawn would make their weight known. What did Colt *want* him to do?

"We've got to take the wise guy with us," Suds advised from the doorway. "He's got too much mug . . ."

"Step up and walk ahead of me," Shank interrupted. "And no yelling, or I'll bust your heads in. You too, wise guy," he looked at Vance.

When Shank took his eye off Colt, he leaped. His left caught Shank under the jaw. The gangster tottered off balance backward. Before he could retaliate, Colt's second blow opened his cheek, and a third his nose. Vance tore in to help knock Shank to the floor, but too late. Suds, screaming to Shank to get out of the way, fired twice.

Savey nodded all right to Hobey, who wanted him to take a message to Vance, and left the Assembly Room. He bounded up the stairs for he didn't want to miss a minute of the exciting events below. He had almost reached the door of the Lav before the noise penetrated. Then he heard two revolver shots.

Three steps brought him into view of the carnage. He

saw a smallish stranger dancing around with a revolver in one hand and screaming, "Let me at him . . . let me at him."

Savey did not let his usual inability catch up with impulse. He leaped at the dancing figure from the rear with more fury than calculation. Suds crashed. The revolver sounded. Savey knocked it out of the limp hand and took Suds by the throat in a giant's grip. While he squeezed, he pounded Suds' head up and down on the floor. He had no clear thought, nothing but a savage passion to end this threat. In the blurred region three feet away the furious thrashing of bodies went on . . .

*　*　*　*　*

Already the wait was embarrassing. The Assembly Room was filled to capacity with restless boys. On the platform, Hobey and Brick, Tracy and Bellman sat in the uncomfortable limelight. Master Harty looked again at the clock. Quarter past eight. It was incomprehensible. No candidate had ever been late to this particular rite in Harty's memory. It wasn't a good way to solicit votes. Harty saw Steve, obviously anxious also, by the door and said, "Do you mind going to remind your roommate that he's wanted? We'll wait patiently here until breakfast time, but not a minute later."

A universal groan rose at this witticism, and Steve left. Henry Vanner rose in the rear and said, "I'll go help Steve."

"Thank you, Henry," Harty said, "Don't come back without your man."

Harty had ways of taming impatience and said, "Boys sometimes go wrong in one way or another. I want to tell you about one who was inclined to wickedness and even, in a quiet way, practised it."

After this promising opening, the boys suffered Harty to

while away another ten minutes. But they all were wondering with part of their minds what had happened to Colt, and finally what had become of Steve and Master Henry. Then sounds at the rear doors caused everyone to look. There stood the dean of boys and Steve with as unexpected an outfit as even Harty's vivid imagination could contrive. Harty said quickly, "I thought my story was sufficiently bloody, but here I see we've got the real thing. Come forward, please."

Henry Vanner led the way with Shank. Steve brought Suds. Colt and Vance and Savey followed. All five had blood on their faces and wore tatters for clothes. They lined up in front of the platform while the silenced roomful stared. Master Henry said, "I know you boys want to get to the voting, so I'll make this account short."

"No! No! Don't," shouted a hundred throats, and Harty added, "Not *that* short, anyway, Henry."

Vanner held up a hand and the silence was instant. "By now we all know in a general way that Colt belonged to a reputable street club in Brooklyn called the Hi-Gunners. When law-breaking gangsters took the club over, Colt tried to resign, and did leave, but was pursued. We are proud of the boy, now in this room, who was instrumental in rescuing Colt from the clutches of the gangsters who were carting Colt off to a so-called trial and undoubtedly saved his life."

"Neil! Neil MacQuarrie!" sang out several boys and everybody shouted.

Harty silenced the room and Henry Vanner went on, "Today two members of the gang came out here to kidnap Colt. Vance noticed these strangers ranging around the second floor dorm and kept an eye on them. They stumbled on

Colt in the Lav and ordered him and Vance to accompany them down the fire escape to their car. Colt knew that his plight involved harm to Vance, and probably his death. Colt offered to go if they'd spare Vance, but their leader, this big man here named Shank, dared not risk that. So nothing was left but resistance.

"Colt jumped into Shank, with Vance following. This other gangster, Suds, was stationed in the doorway. Shank tells me that he ordered Suds to threaten with his revolver but not to fire. Suds got panicky when he saw Shank downed, and fired twice as best he could at the struggling combatants in the hope of hitting Colt or Vance without killing Shank.

"Savey was hurrying to summon Vance when he reached the Lav door, saw Suds dancing around with revolver in air, waiting for a clear shot at Colt or Vance. Savey charged Suds, ended the revolver threat, and pounded Suds unconscious . . ."

The roomful of boys could stand the tension no longer and roared "Hooray for Savey!" "Fine work, Savey!" "Good for Savey!"

Harty silenced them again and Vanner said, "Colt and Vance had the situation in hand before Steve and I reached them. The place looked like a slaughterhouse. Our boys had frisked the attackers of knives and guns. Shank had told Colt that the plot had been hatched in a Village resort known to us all. Colt sent Steve, armed, to apprehend the gangster waiting in the car, while Savey phoned the police. A patrol car happened to be near, and the law has made arrests in the Village and has the car driver. Savey and I did our best to swab down the wounded, and here we are."

Master Harty quelled new applause by crying out, "I

yield! I feared Master Henry's story would be better than mine. In my story I go along with only one hero. But here we have three, large as life and bloody as a battlefield. Boys, I suggest we give salvos for them starting with Vance.

The roars arose and terminated with "Vance, Vance, *Vance!*"

Then "Savey, Savey, *Savey!*"

Then "Colt, *Colt,* COLT."

Harty went on, "I don't know a better place to keep Messrs. Shank and Suds until the police take over than right here."

Yells of agreement broke out and had to be suppressed. "You boys have had your fill of staring at four of the candidates, no matter how beautiful they are. Now take a quick look at the other one while the ballots are being passed. We can do the voting here."

The other candidate stood there in his blood and rags and found the inspection almost as trying as being confronted by armed Hi-Gunners. The skin had been knocked off his prominent nose, his lips were swollen. But the deep eyes and fine head were steady. It was Harty's cleverest move to give Colt a boost, thought Manager Ian, who was deeply impressed anew.

Harty ended the difficult minute by saying, "That'll do, Colt. Another time, please don't keep the voters waiting."

A roar of laughter marked this injunction. "Good old Harty," Kress said to Cecil Maxton. "He knows his boys, and how! The light touch and a tight grip. That's all it takes—if you care enough."

*   *   *   *   *

Dear Ike, Harty wrote a week later.

Law and order won. Colt was elected Student Body President by the largest majority of any candidate in my memory. You'll have as fine and upstanding a young man to head Council as any Ironwood has been privileged to mold.

Colt is nineteen and has had a toughish life, as I've written you. But good blood is heaven's best gift, and when it's Scottish blood as well, you have someone who knows how to use the gift.

I've been hard on the boy, I admit. He's behind in his studies and needed all his time to prepare for Cornell. But I feared another weak S.B.P. (Hobey Tyler) if Colt didn't run. So I appealed to him. He had to have Council experience, of course, and Kress got him to play ball. This came near being a boomerang.

But his past history stepped in, and because it was a good history, it saved him. Our arch enemy Alcibiades was sore at Colt for stopping the cigarette traffic from his den. He notified Colt's enemies, the Hi-Gunners described in the newspaper clipping I sent you, of his presence at Ironwood. Two gangsters came, saw, and were conquered. Vance Draper's innate decency took charge and he acted heroically in combat. The once meek Savey Miller throttled the second gangster himself. Savey is definitely ex-chrysalis.

Ellen Waring is again the girls' S.B.P. As she and Colt are extremely happy together, and a dual force for good, I think Ironwood will keep the Commandments. Brick

Evans will head the Work Program, and Steve Livey will be Chief Proctor. They don't come better.

Your plan to appear unannounced on Commencement Day is dandy and the secret will be kept. Robert MacQuarrie, the father of Ian and Neil, has consented to be speaker—a load off my mind. You needn't fear that this year of scepter-wielding will tempt me to usurp the throne. Uneasy does lie the head that wears the crown. But, as my youngest says, it's been awful fun.

Yours devotedly,
Harty.